Magenta Opium

by
Sharon Baillie

New Libri Press

All rights reserved under International and Pan-American Copyright Conventions. No part of this book may be reproduced, transmitted, downloaded, decompiled, reverse engineered, or stored in or introduced into any information storage and retrieval system, in any form or by any means, whether electronic or mechanical, now known or hereinafter invented, without the express written permission of the publisher.

This is a work of fiction.
Nothing is in it that has not been imagined.

Copyright © 2013 by Sharon Baillie

Cover Art by Sharon Baillie
Cover Copyright © 2013 by New Libri Press

ISBN: 978-1-61469-033-7

Published in 2013 by New Libri Press
Mercer Island, WA 98040
www.newlibri.com

New Libri Press is a small independent press dedicated to publishing new authors and independent authors in both eBook and traditional formats.

In no particular order:

For David.

For Jonathan.

For Petra.

Contents

Chapter, the First — Spilled Milk	9
Chapter, the Second — Watership Down Below	14
Chapter, the Third — Ta2	19
Chapter, the Fourth — Degree, the Second	23
Chapter, the Fifth — Academically Challenged	27
Chapter, the Sixth — Rabbit Stew	32
Chapter, the all-important Seventh	36
Chapter, the Interlude: Eighth	39
Chapter, the Ninth — Yes	43
Chapter, the Tenth — Progress	47
Chapter, the Eleventh — Schmental	51
Chapter, the Twelfth — Suspicious Minds	54
Chapter, the Thirteenth — Showdown At The BS Corral	58
Chapter, the Somethingth — Magenta Morphean Delight	62
Chapter, the Fifteenth — Plan A	64
Chapter, the Sixteenth — Previously, in Magenta Opium	68
Chapter, the Seventeenth — Conversation With The Dead, Part I	71
Chapter, the Eighteenth — Conversation Over The Dead	75

Chapter, the Nineteenth — Concurrent Events	80
Chapter, the Twentieth — Road Trip	86
Chapter, the TwentyFirst — The Promotion	89
Chapter, the TwentySecond — Family Values	94
Chapter, the TwentyThird — Salt & Pepper	98
Chapter, the TwentyFourth — Conversations With Beelzebub	104
Chapter, the TwentyFifth — Love Life	110
Chapter, the TwentySixth — Collision Course	114
Chapter, the TwentySeventh — Very Demotivational	119
Chapter, the TwentyEighth — Not For The Faint-Hearted	123
Chapter, the TwentyNinth — Conversations With Villains	127
Chapter, the Thirtieth — When Worlds Collide	131
Chapter, the ThirtyFirst — From A Whisper…	134
Chapter, the ThirtySecond — Sunday. Bleeding Sunday	138
Chapter, the ThirtyThird — Love Is A Verb	142
Chapter, the ThirtyFourth — Fate's a Bitch	146
Chapter, the ThirtyFifth — The Duality of Time	150
Chapter, the ThirtySixth — All's Well	153
Chapter, the ThirtySeventh — Nuptially Yours	156
Chapter, the ThirtyEighth — Good For The Soul	159
Chapter, the ThirtyNinth — For Completeness	162
Chapter, the Fortieth — Conversation With The Dead, Part II	167
Chapter, the FortyFirst — The First Day	172
Chapter, the FortySecond — 42	176

Acknowledgments

The words "thank you" are insufficient to convey the extent of gratitude due to my family for their love and support. I am the woman I am today because of every day spent with you guys. You make being a wife and mother so easy that I have time to write novels – who could ever want more? David, Jonathan and Petra, you are the best.

For John Bishop (not the comedian, the funny one that I know) thank you for your professional eye when I needed it. Look how grown up we are now! Lawyers, scientists, authors etc.

Martyn Miller, thank you for your photographic skills for the book cover. Like a boss!

Michael Muller, my New Librian, thanks for not objecting to too many Scottish/made up words. And thank you for helping me bring Magenta Opium to the masses.

On a technical note, my thanks go to Blackberry for making a phone that I could write an entire novel on while commuting. How cool are you guys!

Finally, thank you Mum for the writing gene.

And Dad for making me believe that I could do anything in the universe: I'll see you in heaven.

Chapter, the First
Spilled Milk

The girl who lost her mother 8 years, 4 months and 17 days previously – lost her mother in the literal not euphemistic sense – dropped the glass in her hand. It fell on its edge, bounced once, spilled its contents (milk) and cracked down the length. She briefly contemplated crying (but what's the point?). The noise that startled her into dropping the glass roared again as she lifted it from the floor. She kept hold of the glass and contemplated the noise before tears. It sounded like thunder in the living room. She was currently in the kitchen, broken glass in hand, milk seeping at her toes. And again, the thunder. This time with a rat-a-tat-tat. Was it the door? Could a door make that amount of racket and still stay a door and not become kindling? Were its hinges still intact or would they shear through with another attack? If it was the door. Their door had never caused even an ounce of trouble, why would it start now? Her dry toes got itchy for milk. Everything must be even. Milk seeping at the right toe must be equalled with milk on the left. There's also a temperature issue. Likewise with the door, although able to be a door at standard temperatures and pressures, its door-like qualities are not altogether independent of temperature. At 800 degrees (Celsius or Fahrenheit, choose your poison) the door would be a doorway plus mess. At -200 it would be a wall; immovable. This is precisely why the Inuits didn't invent alloyed metals. She switched feet, resting her dry toes close enough to the spill to begin to draw up the moisture. The milk was 20 degrees Celsius, give or take 2 degrees Kelvin.

The girl who lost her mother (literally, not euphemistically) had just put the glass – broken, empty, wretched glass – on the sink when the door thundered again. She was sure that time it was a door noise. Although what the door had to be so noisy and angry about she couldn't guess. Maybe tinkers were after the letterbox again. Stolen letterboxes were assumed to be a thing of the past, but people still blogged about theirs being taken. Tinkers were the prime suspects. What would drug addicts want with a letterbox? Nothing. Tinkers were to blame. The door was delighted when she opened it; it had enjoyed being pounded a little more than being pulped.

Turns out it was the police. Shiny buttons, gelled hair, numbers on shoulders stood before the girl, now a woman, who literally lost her mother when she was still a girl. Did police steal letterboxes? Who would suspect them? The tinkers might, but who would listen to a letterbox-thieving race? Her letterbox remained attached to the now happy door as it should, ready to receive tomorrow's special offers for the Co-op and plastic bags for disused toys. Miserable but safe letterbox. If the police weren't trying to steal the letterbox what did they want? Did police steal whole doors? The milkdamp-toed woman peeled her socks off while the shiny buttons spoke.

'My dad's not here,' Veronica said.

'How old are you?' one of them asked.

'Twenty two last February.'

They muttered.

'I'm not a retard,' she said, milkdamp socks in hand, milklessdamp toes wriggling.

'What will we do, Sarge?'

While Sarge was contemplating what to do, Veronica was contemplating the broken glass. What would dad say? She didn't know so instead she contemplated letters that were numbers. Numbers that had names were practically perfect in every way. Avagadro's number answered questions people never thought to ask. But it knew the answers anyway. How many molecules in your fingernails, how many atoms in a cornea, how much sugar in a teaspoon of sugar, what percentage of table is table and how much is outer space.

'Do you have a computer?'

'No,' Veronica answered, 'I use the computer at university.'

'Does your dad have a computer?'

'At work.'

The shouldered buttons spoke amongst themselves, 'are you sure this is the right place', 'can't trust these beautiful mind types', 'slow', 'double check', 'check'. Meanwhile cold toes became milkcrusted.

'When will your dad be home?'

'Soon. What will he say about a broken glass?'

'Was it an accident?'

'Of course, why would I break it on purpose? Do people break glasses on purpose?'

More muttering, 'be very sure', 'litigation'.

'Miss, we're going to come back later.'

Eight years, 4 months and 18 days precisely previously (for a night had passed since the police first called) Veronica had lost all her baby teeth but not a mother. She went to school motherful and came home motherlost. It was her 14th birthday. There was a cake in the cupboard with Teletubbies on it. The girl with a lost mother and the husband with a lost wife had cake for dinner. Tinky Winky, Dipsy, Lala and Po instead of Thursday macaroni.

'We never need to have macaroni again,' the wifelost man said when they inspected their wardrobe to find it devoid of her.

'Why is she gone?' Veronica asked.

'I don't know.'

'Will she be back?'

'Probably not,' was the only discussion needed by either the motherlost or the wifelost. There was no void left or felt but all the same Mr Dempsey, with a wife physically lost, filled it by paying someone to fill the void he didn't really have.

Veronica barely noticed the difference, except that dad went out more and came home smelling like under the sink did that time a mouse died back there and flies laid eggs in its rotting stomach. The motherlost girl made a graph and found a linear relationship between how rotten her dad smelled with how happy he was. Extrapolating it back to zero the conclusion was there to be drawn that every day until 8 years, 4 months and 18 days previous he had smelled faintly of clean skin and therefore was totally miserable, but Veronica didn't make the graph to draw conclusions, but just because she wanted to.

The void that wasn't really there that he paid a big-strapping-woman to fill was not filled with sex. Not in the classical sense of the word sex. No copulation was involved. Big-strapping-tattooed-woman would take wifelost husband in her specially adapted flat and … It's not time yet for that.

The morning after the police first visited they called again. The door was less traumatised, the letterbox un-threatened and Mr Dempsey – petrified they knew about big-strapping-tattooed-rough'n'tumble-woman transactions – invited them in with a guilty quiver which was noted by all shiny buttoned gel headed shoulder numbers, since that was their job. Again they asked about computers.

'We don't have one at home,' he said, 'I use the one at work at lunchtime to read the BBC news. Veronica, my daughter, has never asked for one. Of course, you're welcome to look around.'

The black figures moved from room to room like corporeal clumsy shadows. They removed towels out the airing cupboard, looked under Veronica's bed, searched the electricity happy shed and gathered in the kitchen muttering: 'absolutely sure', 'no question', 'hiding something', 'keep looking', 'guilty'.

They searched again because it was their job and they were 'absolutely sure'.

'We'll need to check the loft,' Mr Dempsey was told.

'I don't have a ladder, I'll get a chair.'

Chair retrieved, a thick, touchable excessively hair-gelled shadow opened the loft while Veronica watched from the bathroom doorway. White plastic ladders incorporated into the loft hatch slid down and stopped on the chair.

'That's odd,' Mr Dempsey said, surprise and guilt (about completely unrelated rough'n'tumble-woman matters) mixed in equal measure, 'we don't have loft ladders.'

And so, precisely 8 years, 4 months and 18 days after she was lost, Veronica Dempsey's mother was found.

Chapter, the Second
Watership Down Below

Mrs Jessica Dempsey (nee Smyth with a y) had a vibrant and well-nurtured online persona. Her facebook, myspace and twitter pages all showed a picture of Jessica Rabbit: her myspace status constantly read 'im not bad im just drawn that way' (*sic*), which, aside from lacking any punctuation becoming it was factually incorrect twice. She was bad. She wasn't drawn. Her last facebook update before the computer in the loft was removed as "evidence" read 'shit the fuzz'. 13 people liked this, 8 people commented but none of the comments commented that the status would have benefitted from a comma.

The fuzz took 3 hours to remove "evidence" from the loft. Boxes were filled and passed through the hatch with the nifty new plastic stairs: when did they get there, seriously? Mrs Dempsey sat on the toilet and contemplated her lost Shangri-La till they were finished. Mr Dempsey sat on his bed and contemplated his potential loss of Shangri-La till they were finished. Veronica Dempsey offered to help pass boxes but was told to wait with her dad and contemplate whatever sort of thing she cared to contemplate until they were finished. She contemplated the possibility of her mother being a letterbox thief.

'All that time,' her dad said, 'in the loft.'

It didn't sound like letterbox-filled boxes being passed through the plastic loft hatch.

'All those years, in the loft, and we didn't even know.'

The neighbours had seen Mrs Dempsey coming and going for the last 8 years, 4 months and 18 days as normal, but hadn't bothered to mention this normal behaviour to anyone as Mr Dempsey and Veronica hadn't bothered to tell them she was lost.

Twenty-three boxes filled with illegal loft content were stacked in a fuzz van. Jessica Non-Rabbit was taken away quietly; she had nothing to say to the offline world. The motherfound woman, once a motherlost girl, and wifefound man, happy and pungent wifelost man the day before, were 'taken in for questioning'.

Veronica did the questioning: 'does my mum steal letterboxes? Do the police sometimes steal letterboxes? Ever? Do people that break glasses go to jail? Is she going to prison? How big is a cell? Will she have internet? Will it be just like the loft, small and with the internet? How did she get internet in the loft? What's worse, stealing letterboxes because you're a tinker or being a drug addict and not stealing letterboxes? When can we go home?'

'You have things to do?' they asked.

'Of course.'

Mr Dempsey asked about the illegal content of the boxes and was asked about the illegal content of the boxes.

'Do you really expect us to believe your wife lived in your loft for almost 10 years without your knowledge?'

'Yes.'

'Did you report her missing?'

'No.'

'Did you keep her in the loft against her will?'

The shiny buttoned fuzz knew the answer to all the questions they asked but asked them all twice anyway.

'Do you *expect* us to believe your wife lived in your loft for almost a decade without your knowledge?'

'Yes.'

They did.

They let the wifefound man – sad in the finding – and the motherfound woman – wholly indifferent – home in time for dinner. They kept bad Jessica along with 23 boxes of loft-salvaged illegalness longer.

'Will mum be living in the loft when they let her out?' Veronica asked.

'Maybe they won't let her out,' Mr Dempsey said optimistically.

*

Eight years, 4 months and 18 days previously Jessica Dempsey (nee Smyth – don't forget the y! –) had a plan ready for action. She packed her belongings and went to the train station where she boarded the 10:03 to King's Cross, London. She navigated her suitcased self to a prearranged hotel and waited for her one and only true love (that she met in an internet chatroom 4 months earlier). Firm_Buttock_Pete. A cyclist. He sent photos of his firm buttocks in lycra, 'not bad for a 45 year old.jpeg'. Firm_Buttock_Pete showed up with proudly firm buttocks, which he proudly showed off.

The worldwideweb was a cub in those days, meowing slowly through dial-up, disconnecting at the whim of the internet gods with a purr and a clickclick, meanwhile unobtrusively taking over the world. It supplied the proles and elite and companies and governments, all of which predated it with sufficient aplomb, with enough interpium (internet opium) to leave every man Jack of them sweating urine and vomiting organs at even the prospect of its withdrawal: it mutated and assimilated life as it was to life as it wanted.

Firm_Buttock_Pete was an original dial-up predator before it occurred to people to be wary about meeting strangers that they had literally never met before in strange places without letting anyone know where they would be. Fortunately for Jessica all he wanted was a go of her. Unfortunately for Jessica all he wanted was a go of her. Unfortunately for Jessica he wasn't very good. But fortunately for Jessica he wasn't very good. Less than an hour after the awkwardness of meeting her one and only and forever true love for the first time – dear internetgod, what an annoying lisp! Is his back crooked? What the hell does his face do that for when he speaks? Interesting smell, sort of garlic infused with brimstone, probably exactly what Hades would smell like if Greek gods were still alive – he left.

Time to amend the plan.

An hour older, an hour less naïve but timelessly stupid, Jessica – who now considered herself a SmYth again – re-navigated in reverse her suitcased self to King's Cross train station, London, whereupon she boarded a train to the place that morning she called home. The amended plan could have consisted of unpacking and acting like nothing untoward had happened that day. Instead, the amended plan consisted of living in the loft, unknown by downstairs cohabiting husband and daughter. Neither were that bright. None were that bright. Over the years the loft space went from musty and uninhabitable to musty with a middle-aged hormone deficient being habiting it.

As Jessica Dempsey (nee Smyth and currently self considered as Smyth) secluded herself from the world her interpium habit grew, flourished, grew some more and then flourished. Internet chatrooms made way for social networking sites. Sleeping or awake, MSN was always open. Jessica Rabbit lived wholly on-line. She earned money by taking off her bra for the benefit of anyone with a credit card who wanted to look at a braless middle-aged hormone deficient woman. On the internet that numbered in the thousands. She also downloaded Hollywood, Bollywood, independent and assorted movies which she burned to disc and sold to a market stall for cash. The police had little interest in the braless Rabbit but took great offence to the copyright breaching.

Which is why, 8 years, 4 months and 18 days after being duped by an internet whore into internet-blessed (but over in minutes) union, Mrs Dempsey (as the fuzz insisted on calling her) was arrested for peddling DVDs; some good, some rubbish, some scary, some rude, some funny, some cartoons, some violent, some surreal, some soppy, and every last one of them very and completely illegal.

Chapter, the Third
Ta2

Thirteen days after the shiny-buttoned numbered-shoulder fuzz first called, that is to say, 12 days after their second call and removal of mothersquatter by her Majesty's command for questioning about 23 containers of illegal internet activity (braless internet activity deliberately ignored with a shudder and a gag), that is to say further, 11 days after she was returned and took position back in the loft in a non-secret capacity ('I have nowhere else to go'), Veronica Dempsey embarked upon her second degree. Also, on the exact self same day, that is to say for clarity, 13 days after visit 1 of the fuzz, 12 days after visit 2 and 11 days after The Return of The Rabbit, the prodigal son/brother returned and retook his room ('I have nowhere else to go').

The relofted mother remained as uninterested in everyone's lives as she had been when she was loftlost and blatantly uninterested. Interpium (*inter*net o*pium*, take note this time!) withdrawal was tough on the mildly afflicted; on Jessica Offline it was practical destruction. She shook, sweated, fingers twitched constantly, typing words on invisible keyboards, greetings, quips, lol, updating statuses ('shaking and sweaty'), typed AFK, BBS nowhere.

Proctor Dempsey, the aforementioned prodigal, was a full decade older than his sister Veronica and hadn't been seen or heard from in a full decade. He returned unaware that his mother had been lost, by choice, for 8 years, 4 months and 18 days, only to be reinstated officially into the home a mere 11 days earlier.

'Why does mum live in the loft?' he asked his dad.

'It suits her,' he replied.

'Why does mum live in the loft?' he tried the same question on Veronica.

'She didn't say,' she replied.

It was Proctor who first alerted Veronica to the heinous crime of letterbox thievery, from firsthand experience or not she was too young to ponder, but not too young to worry about her sad letterbox. She knew the letterbox to be sad because it carried the mood of everything put through it: satin-look letters peddling credit; menus for the local Asian takeaway cuisine establishments with generic pictures of burgers (the letterbox was sad for the Dempseys because the burgers never looked like the pictures); council tax bills; phone bills; electricity bills; sugar bills; lawyers' letters; begging letters from MPs; money-off coupons for products they never bought, dreary, dreary, dreary, and once, but only once, excrement.

On that occasion tinkers thieving it would have been a blessed relief.

'So, little sister, you're at uni now?' Proctor sat on her bed and interrupted her reading.

'I've been at uni for 4 years.'

'I always thought you were so dumb you were probably supersmart with it.' He looked through her books without looking at her books. He never stole any letterboxes, he didn't pirate movies and sell them for profit, but he had broken the law in his own quaint little way. He battered people, without their consent, for a nice volume of money. To begin with he battered people, with their consent, for a lesser volume of money. He was gifted in the boxing ring and his greatest asset – complete ignorance of consequences – had got his talent noticed and his head headhunted by the sorts of people that pay masses of money to have unconsenting people battered, the sorts of people your mother would have warned you about if she knew anything about mothering (and less about piracy of the non-aaaarghmatey variety), the sorts of people that bang on about 'honour' and 'loyalty' and feed each other to circular saws, the sorts of people you don't put on your CV under Previous Employers nor Character References (especially not as Character References!), the sorts of people that keep keepsakes from other people's keepsakes collections, the sorts of people that association with will end you up in jail. Proctor Dempsey had just finished 3.5 years in the big house for a battering he inflicted leaving the batteree in a coma for, coincidentally, 3.5 years. After his life hiatus the batteree moved to New Zealand where, in time, he would develop skin cancer but, thanks to the hard work by the Cancer Researchists, he would survive. The balance of his life would be evened. After his life hiatus the batterer returned to his childhood home, the balance of his life still out of kilter. He wanted a plan. A killer plan. A distraction plan. He wasn't smart enough. So he plagiarised a plan. He would learn origami and tattoo his upper body like Michael Schofield of Prison Break fame[1]. He was quoted £2500 for the ink. He was also quoted £800. He went for the £800 quote although neither quoter nor quotee knew what they were undertaking. He sat in the faux leather tattoo chair for 12 hours and bled and cried for 11 hours 58 minutes of it.

Veronica rubbed cream made for nappy rash all over his torso. He bled and cried through it all. She wrapped him in clingfilm and he still bled and still cried.

---

[1] Michael Schofield is a fictional character, and a card-carrying genius, who had the blueprints of a fictional prison, Fox River, tattooed in code on his upper body for reasons that the real title of the fictional television series more than subtly allude to: Prison Break. The television series was created by Paul Scheuring and starred Wentworth Miller and Dominic Purcell, with a show-stealing performance by Robert Knepper as 'T-Bag'. This 20th Century Fox Home Entertainment masterpiece can be bought under the ASIN B0023N-VA92.

'Fox River is a fictional prison,' she said as she worked.

'So?'

'So you can't use these plans to help you escape from prison.'

He bled and cried for longer, 'Escaping from prison is for pussies. Real men do their time[2].'

'How much time did you spend in prison?' she asked.

'What makes you think I've been to prison?'

She finished wrapping his bleeding, leeching ink, nappy-rash creamed body; red, black and yellow mushed below a plastic skin. 'You're different and not just older.'

'What's your darkest secret?' he asked as she left him to quietly ooze out.

'Don't have one,' she said. At that point, of course, she hadn't killed.

---

[2] In the television series Prison Break there is a death penalty to contend with, hence the allegation that escaping from prison is for pussies is not applicable and Michael Schofield is not being called a pussy in the text. Proctor Dempsey's statement is only relevant in a judicial system that does not employ capital punishment.

Chapter, the Fourth
Degree, the Second

The earth precessed around the sun at precisely the correct speed to remain in its orbit and not veer off course and either freeze everyone solid in a microsecond or boil mankind effervescently in a picosecond. Time, such as the scientists would have the lay person believe, ebbed forward linearly, no pauses, no deviations, not even for those in love. Flowers slept at night, night after night after night after night. Foxes invaded towns at night, every night, most nights feasting, some nights (but only once per fox in general) they lost a deathrace with a car's headlights. Days passed more slowly to Veronica Dempsey than nights but she knew that was just her perspective of it; the earth's speed was constant and its trajectory perfect for the world to stay Earth. As for her New-FoundMum living in the loft, every rotation of the Earth was a long struggle that led her towards a trial date. Veronica Dempsey gave her no thinking time. Proctor Dempsey got a job as a bouncer when his bleeding stopped and his scabbed scabs, rescabbed, picked, itched, oozed yellow body mucus, rescabbed and eventually fell off. His tattoos looked like he'd paid someone £800 to do a job worth £2500. His secret Fox River map was defective as a means of escape from Fox River penitentiary – aside from the obvious defection of Fox River not existing – with skewed floors, blurred passages and extensive scarring at the most scratched at areas, but scared the shit out the average Joe. He battered the average Joe in an official capacity as and when necessary. He lived a crepuscular life and found the nights longer than the days. His plagiarised plan had not gone exactly to plan. His life was still out of kilter and his origami attempts looked like they'd been made by the kids from the special school that the other kids from the special school called 'retards'. Veronica Dempsey allowed some thinking time for him because he made more noise than her mother. Mr Dempsey's inversely proportional smell/happiness graph nosedived towards miserable as his aroma improved. He smelled like soap and skin, he never went out on an evening but waited in miserable suffocating sanitary skin for his wife to hopefully go to jail. He offered himself as a character witness against her. His withdrawal from big-strapping-woman was a hygienic improvement but left his brain unfocussed on 'important things' like people crossing the road when he was driving and counting money properly when working (something the bank easily got on their high horse about when it didn't happen to their 'standards'). All he wanted was to feel the touch of her rough ... It's not time for that yet. Veronica Dempsey didn't give him any thinking time because it was unnecessary to think about routine.

What she did think about was her second degree. Her first degree, she didn't have to think about; routine getting up, routine classes, routine tutorials, routine exams, routine lunch, routine labwork, routine matriculation number, routine learning, routine living, routine sleeping, routine reading, routine questions, routine queuing, routine pencils, pens, markers, rubbers, rulers, set squares, sharpeners, pencil cases, coppers, periodic table, routine calculations, routine answers, routine cooking, routine weekends, routine Monday-Friday, routine seats in routine classrooms, routine birthdays, routine avoidance, routine lack of socially necessary interactions. That's not to say that routine is humdrum. Routine is just routine. Anything more and it's not routine. Routine

First Class (Hons) Bachelor's Degree in Chemistry, not a Humdrum First Class (Hons) Bachelor's Degree in Chemistry. Routine First Class first degree in the bag, Veronica Dempsey began her second degree on the day her prodigal (but unpenitent) brother returned.

'Good luck today,' her dad said, 'I'm so proud of you.'

Before the miracle, or freak genetic mutation (pot-ae-to, po-tah-to), of Veronica, the Dempseys and Smyths and all generations leading up to the union of Dempsey with Smyth had been "academically challenged", to use the accepted phraseology. They were "thick as 2-day old lentil soup", to not use the accepted phraseology. Veronica Dempsey (BSci, First Class (Hons (Routine))) was also thick as 2-day old lentil soup, but with almost total recall. Routine reading material could be recalled without searching through masses of unrelated reading material stored electronically in her supercomputerbrain. Everything was filed and categorised in conveniently retrievable filing cabinets in her mind, cross-referenced extensively. Thus Veronica Dempsey gave the impression of 'intellect' with high academic scores whilst being almost entirely socially inept. She was practically born for a life in academia where her obsessive attention to routine was sought, encouraged and rewarded with certificates that said things like, 'Veronica Dempsey has achieved an excellent standard in Practical Laboratories' and 'Veronica Dempsey has achieved Above Average scores in all exams', but what they all could have said was, 'Stone the crows, that girl can remember stuff really really well'.

So, on the day Proctor Dempsey returned ('I have nowhere else to go') having just been released from Her Majesty's Pleasure, Veronica Dempsey changed routine. To the never innocent bystander it would appear a superficial change of routine; same routine waking time, same routine ablutions, same routine breakfast, same routine route, same routine university building inhabited from 9 till 6, same ... The 9-6 was new. She used to do 9-5. Within the new 9-6 routine there was barely scope for routine. She did research. Although the act of research was routine and routinely carried out between the hours of 9-6, the actual research evolved on a day-to-day, week-to-week, month-to-month, year-to-year basis; also decade-to-decade, century-to-century and millennia-to-millennia, but that didn't impact on Veronica Dempsey's scheduled 3 year degree period, nonetheless accurate to be pointed out. Experiments could be routinely set up. Predictions could routinely be made, but they will more than routinely be wrong.

'This will work. Crap, why didn't that work? Is the NMR machine working properly? That worked. It didn't work. It did, it will, it must, it should, no reason not to, this derivative worked, that derivative worked, the other derivative. Shit. Wrong colour, wrong shape, way wrong smell, wrong consistency. Turbidity is everything. Is it turbid enough? Crash, damn you, crash, damn you. But slower, damn you. Shit, damn you!'

Unable to fix down, steady out, in short, make routine outcomes from predictable beginnings took its toll on Veronica Dempsey's precarious sanity.

Meanwhile elsewhere the cleaners had been at it again.

Chapter, the Fifth
Academically Challenged

Twenty-two year old, average weight, average height, average brown hair, average brown eyes, average bowel movements, average heart rate, average eyelash length, average top speed, above average recall, less than average social intellect, Veronica Dempsey had never experienced the touch of love. As she was more interested in turbidity than turgidity, this fact was neither here nor there. She hadn't fallen off a mountain either, nor stepped into traffic in full flow, nor learned *Für Elise* on the piano, nor visited the continent, nor ate Marmite, scallops or beef Pot Noodle, nor moved house, nor met a pirate (mother's recent activities notwithstanding, she's never met a pirate of the 'aaaarghmatey' variety), nor played table football, nor baked a baked Alaska, nor complained in a restaurant, nor failed an exam, nor changed a plug, nor been on a motorbike, nor read the Twilight series, nor referred to autumn as fall, nor electrocuted herself either by accident or design, nor kept a goldfish, cat, parakeet or boa-constrictor as a pet, nor dreamt about Simon Cowell. Of all the things she hadn't done, knowing love was just one of them and no more noteworthy than the rest.

Three people shared the research laboratory assigned room 7-14, located on the seventh floor and in the 14th room. It was laboratory like. Formica® benches, white once now splatter decorated with yellow and brown; Formica® floor, white-ish; strip lighting, white glow; beakers, glass; test-tubes, glass; rotary evaporators, white plastic and glass; nitrogen cylinders, brown and grey; paper towels at the sinks, blue; fume hoods for dangerous and smelly chemicals and dangerous smelly chemicals, glass with a red sash; plastic syringes, various sizes, plastic. Various and varied assorted important looking instruments that did not incredibly important things, like shoogle, filled the rest of the space. Veronica Dempsey shared her 9-6 routine with a girl who was also just starting her PhD called Pauline Burns. Pauline Burns smiled a lot with very white teeth and made outlandish claims like, 'I invented hex', 'I lost 9 stone by eating nothing but Cornflakes and honey', and 'I started the internet use of the word pr0n'. She buzzed around, setting up a reaction every so often and buzzed back to her computer. Buzz, reaction, buzz, hometime, buzz, buzz, work, buzz, lunch, buzz, wander about, buzz, smile, smile, buzz, buzz, hair swish, buzz. Buzz. The 9-6 routine was also shared by a male in his final year of PhD study called David Jones. David Jones, known as Davey Jones, not Dave Jones or DJ clucked and hissed and commented: 'that round bottomed flask is as unclean as your mother's conscience'. The girls in the lab had their own ways of dealing with his clucks, hisses and comments. Pauline Burns, all blond hair and white teeth smiled and said, 'so's yer face'. Veronica Dempsey rarely heard the words he said, just clucks and hisses, and the buzzing of Pauline hither to there, and never once replied to a clucked hissed comment.

Laboratory 7-14 (floor 7, room 14, no need for a degree in Numbering to be able to find it) had a small designated writing-up area (technical term) abutting it, designated 7-14A. Veronica Dempsey's desk in room 7-14A, position 1, had a multiracial computer on it. Just a computer. A multiracial computer, but just a computer. Pauline Burns's desk in position 2 had a supremely white computer and a photo of her with someone else. Maybe her boyfriend or maybe the guest star of a cult television series that she met at a convention and paid to have her photograph with that no one would recognise and she could pass off as her boyfriend for the time being and one day say was her husband. It was a glossy photo. It was a toss up. Davey Jones's desk had a laptop. And an ornamental wooden globe. And an alabaster plaque from Benidorm with an eyeless dolphin. And a framed certificate of his 2:1 Degree in Chemistry. And a framed certificate of attending a Microsoft Excel User Course. And a crystal bowl (deep red). And a desk calendar featuring Garfield. And a framed photograph of a beach. And an 8x6 shot of himself running a half marathon six years previously giving the camera two thumbs up. So although his desk (position 3) should have housed his laptop there was no room for it, so it lived on the floor when he didn't need it and on his lap when he did.

'How long do you think you can put your finger in your eye for before it would get sore?' Davey Jones asked them.

'Your eye or your finger?' Pauline asked.

'Your eye or your finger what?' Davey Jones asked.

'Before your eye or your finger would get sore?'

'Your eye. How long do you think you can put your finger in your eye before your eye would get sore?'

Veronica ignored the question and contemplated numbers and atoms and numbers of atoms. Pauline said she didn't know.

'Quite a while,' he said, 'I did it last night, just to see.' It was like an experiment, only without purpose, premise, funding or critical evaluation by a body of his peers. The previous night Davey Jones did indeed put his finger in his eye to see how long it would take to get sore. He ignored the variables of depth, speed, movement and cleanliness of his finger and came to the categorically unscientific conclusion of 'quite a while'. No matter, as he was performing his experiment he was fantasizing about telling Veronica and Pauline about it. In his fantasy they were so impressed by his feat they got down and dirty on the bench adjacent to the rotary evaporator, as most of his fantasies ended these days, two girls and he, stripped, kissing, sweating, doing dirty chemistry outwith[3] a schlenk. All in all the fantasy payoff made the finger-in-the-eye experiment worth it at the time even though there was more chance of knowing the exact velocity and position of an electron simultaneously than there was of ever knowing Veronica and Pauline sexually simultaneously. That is to say, to be specific and official with respect to the electron, there is no chance of ever knowing both, as outlined by the Heisenberg Uncertainty Principle whereby the very act of measuring the velocity or position of the electron interferes to such an extent that the other factor cannot be known with certainty. To be specific with respect to the girls, Pauline had a boyfriend, or certainly said she did, but she also said she invented the colour cyan. Veronica didn't contemplate matters of a sexual nature and wouldn't be talked into it by an amateur debater like Davey Jones. The threesome would never be in spite of increasingly elaborate fantasies from the male in the group who would never give up the idea, even though he didn't particularly fancy either girl.

The three people who shared the research laboratory assigned room 7-14, located on the seventh floor and in the 14th room and the abutting office-cupboard 7-14A all undertook their postgraduate studies under the strict and watchful eye of Dr Barta Savage. Doc Savage was a woman of bronze and the alpha male in most rooms, who liked to shout. Like, *really* liked to shout. On her list of a Few Of Her Favourite Things, being alpha male and shouting would tie for first place. Her shout was impressive. It was the stuff of legends, with a deep resonance and an avalanche-inducing

---

[3] "outwith" – it's a real word, honest. Whilst it may not have common usage outwith Scotland, it is an elegant way to describe something as "outside of, beyond". Incorporate it into your own parlance. The effects may not be as dramatic as saying supercalifragilisticexpialidocious, but you will appear both knowledgeable of other cultures (Scottish) and exceptionally well read (evidently).

tone. If Doc Savage had been a superhero her superpower would have been her voice, which would have been able to tear skin from a living, healthy body with just a whisper. The government would have recruited her and used her on the front line, sitting back and smiling as she levelled armies coming towards her with a lullaby. If she were a superhero, that is. Instead, the shouting at best gave people a fright when they weren't expecting such a noise to come out of a human, and scared the undergraduates into silence during lectures. At worst it probably did once cause an avalanche in Austria resulting in three deaths, but that is unproven and circumstantial.

Doc Savage, not to be confused with the comic book hero with the shared moniker, Doctor Barta Savage, BSc, PhD, MRSC, MRSA, STFU, WTF, LOLX, studied her undergraduate degree at Bath University (no bad thing, no bad thing at all) and her postgraduate studies in Munich where she learned all manner of Germanic habits, like toughening up her w's and banging her mouse on the mousepad when her computer was slow. She engaged in postdoctoral studies in Texas where she learned how to say 'gosh darnit' in place of 'Goddamnit' and 'heck' in place of 'hell', since God, damn and hell are considered 'cuss words' while inhabiting the buckle of the Bible belt.

To say she was formidable is like saying atoms are quite small or the universe is rather large. The atom is unfathomably tiny, and then tinier again, and then even tinier than you can fathom, and the universe head-hurtingly large. No, seriously bigger than whatever you can even imagine. Bigger. Bigger still. Ridiculously bigger than that.

Not even close yet.

Meanwhile elsewhere the cleaners had been at it again.

Chapter, the Sixth
Rabbit Stew

Jessica who had now not been Jessica Rabbit (im not bad im just drawn that way (*sic*)) for seven plus weeks and had been Jessica Offline Dempsey, preferred to be called Smyth with a y, *never* with an i, the woman who left her family for an internet cycling slut but returned home the very same day and hid in the loft for 8 years, 4 months and 18 days before being busted by the fuzz for completely illegally downloading and selling, for profit, copyright material, released on bail to take up residence again in the loft ('I have nowhere else to go') had waited for seven plus weeks for her day in court. Her day arrived without trumpets or heralds, but with a light drizzle and a nervous husband. Proctor Dempsey, the prodigal newly returned son who had 'done time' could have advised his mother on what to wear when going to court to best impress the judge, but he decided to sleep instead. Veronica Dempsey who had never had a run-in with the law and wasn't the most *au-fait* on social conventions probably could still have advised her mother on what not to wear when going to court to be judged by a stranger, but she followed her routine and had left for the lab before her mother was awake. Mr Dempsey alone was available to advise his estranged wife what to wear when going to court, should she feel she needed advice. She had it sorted. After all, she had just spent in excess of seven weeks thinking about what to wear to impress the judge and had settled on a red dress fashioned on the famous white 'Marilyn Monroe standing on a vent, coyly, but ineffectively, holding down her skirt as the updraft lifted it to her neck allthewhile pouting and cooing' dress in the movie Seven Year Itch[4]. It was plunging up top and floaty in the skirt area. It made her feel so good about her aura she even decided to go braless with it, a rather bold and controversial move by a menopausal and sagging woman with a hormone deficiency. Mr Dempsey wanted to hi-five her for her outstanding wardrobe choice but restrained in case he came off as too enthusiastic and she changed into something sane and befitting her day in court.

Jessica's sister Natalie Smyth – divorced, slender, 41, two offspring, WLTM handsome, caring, GSOH male 18-70 with own car and house, smoking an advantage, for nights out to pubs and clubs and maybe more (for 'maybe' read 'defin-feckin-tootly') – arrived at the Dempsey's at 0930 sharp on Court Day with her children scrubbed and spit-shined with the day off school to watch what happens when people use the internet.

'You look lovely, sis,' Natalie said, secretly hi-fiving her sister's psychotic dress sense.

'Ha!' Mr Dempsey thought. The women looked at him. Did he think 'ha!' or did he say 'ha!'? He thought he had thought it. Did he think it aloud? The women were still looking at him. Apparently it was aloud. 'I just remembered something funny I heard one time.'

'Aha,' Mr Dempsey thought more carefully, 'Natalie wants Jessica to go to jail.' His deduction was sound. She did. If the twins got to see their aunt go to jail they might stop asking for a computer ev'ry goddamn minute of ev'ry goddamn day. Cloud, silver lining; Natalie's had one.

---

[4] The Seven Year Itch stars, of course, Marilyn Monroe who, at times, wears a white dress, and can be purchased (the DVD, not the dress) from 20th Century Fox Home Entertainment using the ASIN code B000FKNNAE.

Luke and Leia Smyth (they took their mother's name after the divorce from He Who Shall Not Be Named, The Lying, Cheating, No Good SonUvABitchBastard) sat quietly on the couch while the grown-ups talked about buses and incrimination and boring stuff like that. If they looked at each other very intently they could read each other's thoughts. In actual fact they couldn't, but what they did do was always have exactly the same thoughts as each other at exactly the same time, thereby maintaining the illusion that each could mindread the other. Semantics, really.

'This is boring,' they thought.
'I know, right?' they replied.
'I wonder if she'll go to jail?' they thought.
'That would be exciting!' they replied.
'I wish we had a computer,' they lamented together wordlessly.
'Me too, me too.'

The children were born the wrong way round. Not breach, but the girl was born first. The boy should have been born first. When giving birth to non-single sex twins it's only natural that the boy is born first. Natalie and SonUvABitchBastard never did forgive Leia for being born out of order and Luke for letting her be born out of order. SonUvABitchBastard couldn't live with it and left Natalie and the Wrong Order Twins for the woman with the weight problem and huge tits that works in the cinema. The cinema was his one and only passion and now he got in for free. She was his ideal woman who bore him a son and then after a respectable gap of 18 months a daughter. Meanwhile Natalie cursed him for all his worthless ass was worth (Worthless Cheating Lying No Good SonUvABitchBastardAssFaceBiscuit-Breath) and raised the twins the only way she knew how. By lying to them and telling them Luke was older by eight minutes. She also dressed them like their namesakes from the Star Wars franchise, bleaching Luke's naturally dark hair to blond and darkening Leia's naturally fair hair to chestnut brown. Those goddamn kids couldn't get anything right, born in the opposite order and with opposite hair colour. Deviant from birth, goddamn kids, and what gratitude do you get? 'Mum, can we get a computer? We need to write reports on it for school and it would be good for research.' Computers for doing schoolwork, whoever heard such goddamn backwards kids' nonsense!

'We oughtta go,' Mr Dempsey said.

They went.

The loft sighed a billowing breath as the front door shut behind them all. It could be a loft again, spacious, uninhabited, uninhibited. No longer a refuge for a villain. Lofts are made to keep secrets they don't want to keep: misplaced wives and mothers hiding out there for 8 years, 4 months and 18 days breaking the law, breaking the law, breaking the law. In real life, this life, our life, people don't keep skeletons in closets, they keep skeletons in lofts. Lofts are ageless and knowledgeable. This is why, seven-plus weeks after her arrest when Jessica (please don't call her Rabbit, the loft had seen Jessica Rabbit in action oh, too many times) left the loft and the house the loft knew she would not return to her lofty pirating. The loft knew. The loft was not altogether finished with her yet though.

Jessica, who was forced to acknowledge her current name as Dempsey for the wiggy judge, couldn't understand why he had banged her up when she had worn her special dress. She was given six months; she'd serve three. The judge was seemingly impervious to her twitching nose and wrinkly cleavage. Homosexual. No, asexual. Asexual ruling. Where's the fairness? Jessica Inmate was taken down. She went down looking.

Mr Dempsey sent texts to Proctor and Veronica: Ur mum went to jail. Have a chippy for dinner ill be home late (*sic*).

Chapter, the all-important Seventh

Sometimes, when Veronica Dempsey closed her eyes, there were black people having a meeting inside her head. There was a sunflower yellow mahogany table and daffodil yellow mahogany wood panelling. It was all very 1970s with flares and wide collars and smoking in public. A woman, maternal looking, always took her seat beside an elderly black man with more salt than pepper in his hair and the meeting was ready to begin.

'Things that have the initials VD,' the man said once and those assembled listed Venereal Disease, Vermicelli Daisies, Valentine's Day, Velvet Drawers, Vertical Drop, Violent Demise, Vendredi Dimange, Verrucca Dimples, Victory Day, Vaginal Delivery, Venezuelan Dollars, Vehement Denial, Vanilla Dogs and Victor Drake.

On another occasion the topic raised was, 'Red things you can eat,' and gave forth the list blood, boulders, bile, breath, extract, peppers, tomatoes and strawberries.

She would open her eyes and they were gone. Sometimes she shut her eyes looking for them but they lived in Narnia and could only be found when they weren't being sought.

'Morphine,' he said on yet another occasion, 'discuss.'

'Evil addiction of the druggies, thieving druggies, no good pitiful druggies, dealt a shameful hand druggies.'

'Fields of poppies, gift of God.'
'Pain relief.'
'Assisted suicide.'
'Murder.'
'Overdose.'
'Carbon, nitrogen, oxygen; people, carbon, nitrogen, oxygen; fish, carbon nitrogen, oxygen; dinosaurs, carbon, nitrogen, oxygen; atmosphere, carbon, nitrogen oxygen; morphine, carbon, nitrogen, oxygen; Krebs' Cycle, carbon, nitrogen, oxygen; DNA, carbon, nitrogen, oxygen; life, carbon, nitrogen, oxygen; death, carbon, nitrogen, oxygen; plastics, carbon, nitrogen, oxygen; people, carbon, nitrogen oxygen.'
'The Opium Wars.'
'Heroin.'
'Prostitution.'
'Crack whores.'
'Off topic!' declared the chair. 'Morphine. Discuss.'
'Morpheus, god of sleep.'

Veronica Dempsey, initials VD although not listed at the List Things With The Initials VD meeting, opened her eyes. Morphine. It was a thought. Propositioned by the brain. Postulated by the mind. Drilled down by the subconscious. Refined by the kidneys. Mulled over by the liver. Broken down by the intestines. Cured in the marrow. Developed in the being while Jessica Inmate cried, Proctor Bouncer enpied and Mr Dempsey relieved himself.

There was nothing altruistic about it. There was nothing to it. She searched the scientific literature; hadn't been done yet. Why not? That had been done, this had been done, this that and the other had been done and done again, but not what she was thinking. Why not?

Why hadn't the wheel been invented before it was invented?

The loft constricted when she entered it. It knew what she was planning. It knew the hundred million possible outcomes, statistically speaking half of which ended in failure, and it knew which one she was heading towards. It was helpless to stop her and even if it could have, would it? Why wasn't the wheel invented before it was invented?

While Jessica Lonely aged, Proctor Enpi cried and Happy Dempsey emptied, Veronica Dempsey moonlit. She gathered equipment, clamp stands, clamps, flasks – roundbottom, conical, big, medium, small, tiny, huge – test tubes, pipettes, filter paper and a hotplate to begin with. The loft waited for every new delivery knowing every time she came home with more ferreted goods it lost some of its loftness. The emptiness filled, the loft became a home lab. It wouldn't have stopped her. Why wasn't the wheel invented before it was invented?

Chemicals were tricky beasts. Chemical companies sold morphine but they didn't sell morphine to people. They didn't sell common precursors of morphine to people. A license was needed and quantities were limited and you had to be something more than a person to buy what they sold. Moonlighting Veronica was as patient as the sea and planned how to make morphine from the most basic components. The loft knew it was going to work but it didn't let on. It never exposed its secrets, not the good ones or the illegal ones or the ones the jury is still out on.

Jessica Convict sagged, Proctor Fighter buffed, Satisfied Dempsey smelled and Veronica Dempsey unassumingly but not tentatively took her first steps towards making history while the loft contemplated its dilemma and quietly wept.

Chapter, the Interlude: Eighth

A great leader's shadow weighs no more than a fornicator's. Despite what their flappers would have you believe, a philosopher's weighs no less.

If legends are to be believed – where do legends begin? How reputable is the source? Can the data be validated? Where are the citations? Is a legend told the same twice? Subterfuge is afoot, contortions to fit a moral! – if a legend is to be believed, lightning was called down to settle the debate on the weight of shadows. Shadows were the most intimate part of a man, not like spit, semen or blood which could be given to another, the shadow belonged to him alone and could not be shared with a lover or taken by an enemy. At dusk the shadow stretched and weakened until it faded into nourishing sleep for the next day. If the shadow was an intricate part of man then its weight would testify to the man's great deeds and power. It was all about the power. Two powerful men rose up in central Europe with ambitions of kingdoms, each with an army of a hundred thousand men, each levelled the land they crossed until they crossed each other. They faced off, growled, scrapped and backed away every day for a year. Their strategists saw no weakness in the other. None could triumph so they fought pointlessly for another year. A hundred thousand men on each side became a hundred thousand men in total. Still they faced off, growled and scrapped. A hundred thousand men in total became twenty thousand on each side as another year passed. The powerful leaders stood their ground, their twenty thousand weak army stood beside them, dying by spear and arrow with military regularity until only the two leaders remained. They faced off, growled and scrapped on piles of their dead day after day, neither and none making any significant move on the other. The dead grew bored and trampled. The leaders fought on for another year. The dead decayed and were trampled to slush. The leaders fought.

The legend told, while this legend was forged, was of a witch who had lived for a thousand years on earth, but was of unknown origin (how reputable is the source?). When two hundred thousand men did battle against each other they told stories of her, of her hair made of silver spun into thread, strong as a sword and lethal as hatred. In some stories a male demon mated with a beautiful twisted wench, in others the demon was female who copulated with a murderer (is a legend ever told the same twice?). Her teeth were said to contain venom (can the data be validated?), deadly like an asp. Legend told that she could fly when the moon was full, that she could control the weather at will and she ate human organs (where are the damned citations?).

The witch, who had been taking the spleens of the dead as the leaders slept – the spleens are where the lies are kept and grown; lies nourished the hag – the witch, who had been taking the mouth-smackingly-delicious spleens, was caught defiling the corpses. The powerfully matched duellers called a temporary truce to try, judge and sentence Satan's agent. They contained her power by tying her in ropes fashioned from ambrosia, entwined twice with the tail hairs of a Minatour, dipped in the sea of doubt in the garden of regret.

The witch's eyes burned and countenance heaved as the leaders ponced and pontificated:

'Witch! You ate of our men!'

'Witch! Cursed above all things on earth and below!'

'Witch! Bride of Beelzebub, to him you must return!'

'So say we both, united against you! Your heathery stops here!'

'Vile creature! For the damnation you deserve, we will kill you unto death!'

'May God have no mercy on your soulless form!'

And so the mortal enemies ponced around the captive and pontificated her certain doom. When they grew tired of their speeches, which took many hours as their voices were lullabies to their own ears, they sat and ate together. The Would Be Kings slurped the blood of a deer and smacked tears of its flesh against their cheeks. They devoured the entire beast, sucking up the veins like spaghetti and making tea of its bones, marrow and brain. They shared the eyes – so delicately flavoured compared to the intestines, the eye was sublime! – in the most polite way imaginable, 'oh, you go ahead,' 'why, not at all, you have them,' 'I wouldn't dream of depriving you of the luxury,' 'but I insist,' 'far be it for me to appear selfish over delicacies,' 'they look delicious, you must try them,' 'I'll take great offence,' 'the gods decree you must eat them,' until the hag finally tired of hearing them and squealed 'have one each!'

'Oh my, how silly,' 'of course, we must partake together,' 'what a splendid idea,' 'good show, witch!'

The witch had monitored their battle for 5 years. She – it is only right to refer to the being as a she, although (praise be to God) it was likely 'she' was sterile as a mule and had no genitalia of any description – ate the spleen of the fallen warriors every night for 5 years. She – it's as close a description as any – gorged on their lie-infected organs. She – convention at least dictates we refer to a witch as she – moved among the dead, picking from the plethora of partially decomposed parts. Powerful though she was, everything created has a nemesis. The witch thusly stood bound, with eyes burning at the indignation of it, waiting for her well-feasted captors to kill her unto death.

'I know who is more powerful,' she-it said, moments before they intended to strike her unto death.

In the witch's thousand years she had been working on her most devastating spell, to call down a sword made by the gods, powerful enough to separate man from shadow.

To cut a long legend to a decent length – man alive, some legends can't half go on for a while, almost like they had nothing better to do but sit around telling legends all day long way back when – the witch invented lightning which she controlled with such precision it could schism man from shadow. For the duelling Kings it was useless; their shadows weighed the same. Legend fails to tell of what happened to the witch, but it does say the leftover lightning that wanders the continents searches for her/it/thing/perverse mother creature.

Chapter, the Ninth
Yes

People who have lost limbs cannot be put back together with sellotape. The war-injured, the work-accident victims and those tortured by the use of clippers or chainsaws, with legs, arms, toes, fingers, earlobes, teeth, eyeballs, penises and elbows disattached cannot be reattached by sellotape and told, 'there, there, I'm sure it's not all that bad'. What about gangrene and infection? No, no, sellotape is not the tool for the job. If lightning achieved the maximum power in the flash of a second and managed to, once again, remove a shadow from a lifeform (or non-lifeform, but the lifeform would feel it more profoundly), could it be reattached with sellotape or blu-tac or putty or staples or a bulldog clip or even double-sided-sellotape? Ah, but that is a question leftover from the Interlude! The Interlude is over.

When wifelost mother was found fugitively in the loft, wifefound husband had to curtail his evening excursions with rumpy-pumpy-no-sex-involved woman (temporarily). God damn Jessica, God damn the loft for keeping her. The loft would protest, but the loft is currently occupied with Veronica's Quest. The loft is outside time and houses Jessica Fugitive downloading illegalness at precisely the same time Veronica bubbles and brews Lewis Acids with sexually active Lewis Bases. The Quest is also jam-packed full of illegalness, but the loft is starting to find the smell of this particular brand of law breaking quite mellowing. The sweet, dizzying aroma of toluene has won over the loft. The loft is currently too mellowed out to object. Far out, man.

Mr Dempsey was a lot more traditional than the loft and was only able to consider time linearly (he also believed the fable about blackholes!), as such the loft could only be inhabited by Illegal Wife or Illegal Daughter in chronological order and not co-habiting the same space in different times at the same time. But as he was unaware of any and all illegal activity in the loft, regardless of the physics of the universe, it made no odds. What did make odds was his traditional nature disallowing any evening excursions when Loft Wife was revealed, even though not a blind bit of difference was made. He felt traditionally guilty. The Tuesday prior to the shiny-buttoned-fuzz calling, Jessica Rabbit-If-Only held her domicile in the loft: Mr Dempsey visited his nosexwhore. The Tuesday after gel-haired-shoulder-numbers called, Jessica Computerless held her domicile in the loft: Mr Dempsey stayed home. To paraphrase: Jessica in the loft – Mr D nosexwhore. Following week, Jessica in the loft – Mr D no nosexwhore. Tradition dictated it was poor form to visit your whore, regardless of how little sex was involved, when your wife was living in the same house as you and known to be domiciled there by you as well as the neighbours. Modern thinking individuals would have rationalised it to their conscience *vis-a-vis*; 'the marriage has been over for years, she hasn't even said hello to you, it's as if she's not there, what difference does it make, she was in the loft every other time you went out, she honestly doesn't care, oh my God do you still love her?' Modern thinking caused the cows to go mad and the rabbits to die out. The panda crisis is, admittedly, a product of traditionalism. Swings and roundabouts.

Mr Dempsey, teller at a well-known and equally well-hated bank, met his whore whilst he was tellering. The usual grind of the day was progressing as usual; cheques cashed, direct debits bounced, standing orders out, customers crying, dignity divulged, ordinary looking people with ordinary money problems and ordinary solutions smothered in an extra dose of ordinary made up his ordinary Monday to Friday grind. And then there was her. She was above ordinary height, probably six feet tall, with not very ordinary hair, black at the bottom, blond (almost white) at the top and with flashes of purple. She wore not very ordinary clothes for a visit to the bank, a corset, a black leather corset! Her collarbone was tattooed with a tribal butterfly design, highly out of the ordinary for Mr Dempsey, he'd never seen such a creature outwith modern music videos. And then she was at his till with a wad of Euros and a passport.

'I'd like to open an account, please.'

Where did that voice come from? It sounded like chocolate covered chocolate. Euros? Odd.

He cleared his throat conspicuously, 'Certainly, would you like to come to a desk with me to go over some details?'

'I'll go anywhere with you.'

Mr Dempsey would never be lonely again, for a modest financial outlay. But who can put a price on companionship?

Sellotape cannot be used to reattach limbs, not even the named brand as opposed to the generic supermarket knock-off.

The tall woman did not understand the attraction of regularity. Nor did she judge it. She did whatever suited her best. Recently she had more money given to her than she could spend so it was time to open a bank account. She wasn't conforming. She wasn't a liberal to the point of the ridiculous. She could trust establishments to a degree, as long as it sat well in her kidneys. There were no stress pains over choosing a well-known, if equally well-hated, high street bank. Kidneys were at peace. Liver was unperturbed. She asked to open an account. The kind looking man who was possibly once okay looking, and still had modestly magnificent hair, orally asked her to go to a table with him. Non-verbally he said, 'oh my God, you're the best thing I have ever seen in my life, can you really have walked into my bank? This place isn't worthy of your presence! Aren't there other banks for attractive people to go to? That tattoo is intoxicating. My God, I want to touch you so much! I want to run my hands over your beautiful pale skin. Can I know more about you? Can I know you intimately?'

She heard it all. She said yes.

Chapter, the Tenth
Progress

Interpium spread amongst the weak-minded like an addiction. Jessica Addicted's mind was best described as wishy-washy or 'meh'. Whilst the non weak-minded ran on Mac software, Jessica was still on Windows 95 which crashed every forty seconds or so. Being banged up didn't suit her at all. She had no interest in the politics of the prison; fortunately those who were very interested in the politics of the prison had no interest in her since she was considered soft in the head, or, to use the parlance of the prison, she was a bit of a mental. When she watched TV she said "LOL" instead of actually laughing. She updated her status and mood in a regular sporadic fashion, 'breakfast was mince', 'mood: lethargic', 'can someone please give me three planks for my sheep?' The clearest indication that her brain was operating on 8-bit and completely devoid of Bluetooth technology was that, two days before her three month early release, two months and 29 days into her sentence, she was caught illegally trying to download Dirty Dancing from a file-sharing site. Her defence of, 'Oh come off it, that movie's ancient!' for some reason didn't have the legal weight she expected it would and she was told she'd have to serve her full sentence. 'Mood: hacked off, like, totally.' Mr Dempsey, who neither offline nor online updated his status would, if he did such a thing, have amended his mood to jovial followed by a colon then capital D. What he did do, although rarely, was sing, and he couldn't help but hum his favourite Beatles song about bells on a hill, ringing, 'hm hm hm hm, la la la la, till there was you'. He even performed a modulation.

'What're you so smug about?' Proctor asked.

'Smug? Me? Nothing. I'm not smug. What made you think that I'm smug? Do I seem smug?'

'Well, you know, jovial,' Proctor clarified.

'Jovial? Me? Nah, I'm not jovial. What makes you think I'm jovial? Do I seem jovial?'

Proctor had stopped listening; Veronica hadn't started.

'Anyway, in completely unrelated news,' Mr Dempsey said with smug joviality, 'your mum's being kept in prison longer.'

Veronica wondered how she should react to the news. Her reaction was indifference and she was comfortable with that, but she wondered what the socially accepted, some might call it a "normal", response would be.

'Oh for fuck's sake, that's fucking awful. Bollocks. I fucking miss her.'

She could tell by the gawping brother and dad that she hadn't pitched it right at all. The gawping brother became the hysterical brother who had to hold his sides to keep his internal organs on the internal side, as he laughed out his nose and ears.

'I'm going out,' the gawping father said, and with a final long gawp at Veronica said, 'how about we don't use the f-word in the house?'

Proctor, the respectable job-keeper who still missed beating people up for a lot of money but made do with beating people up for the comparatively small amount he was paid, went to work. Or so he said.

Veronica went to the loft. Why had she even tried to give a socially aware response? That was extremely odd. Maybe the toluene fumes were getting to her. The loft didn't have adequate ventilation for the chemistry she was secretly carrying out in it. The loft itself was constantly high, or else it would be objecting in the strongest terms to getting the blame. Inadequate ventilation. Well, quite. Veronica clearly wasn't being particularly Veronica-like. But the loft had never been more welcoming, warm and deeply aromatic. So she retreated to her clandestine lab and performed illegal Michael additions and contraband Heck coupling reactions while the toluene soaked through her skin, nose hairs, tongue and eyes, coating her brain with molecules to make her dizzy and dipsy.

Inexplicable outbursts aside, the Quest was progressing very well. Shy carbons were encouraged to exchange electrons with needy oxygens; conformations were controlled with an iron fist; rings closed without her even having to swear at them. Well behaved hydrogens rose to the challenge and took up the slack. Atom 1 bonded to atoms 2, 3 and 4. Atom 4 bonded to atoms 1, 5 and 6. Atom 12 was special and refused to be known by any atom other than 13. She was a few weeks away from making morphine, on a small scale and not at all optimised, but a feat nonetheless. Many have tried, but Veronica The Tenacious was going to succeed. Veronica The Patient was going to make morphine. Directly after which Veronica The Genius/Veronica The Insane planned to make morphine better than morphine.

Whilst the elder Dempsey female continued to silently sag in prison and the younger Dempsey female made reluctant double bonds from vivacious single bonds, the elder Dempsey male made his way to a small, respectable cul-de-sac called Gardener Street (a misnomer as it did not lead anywhere, and therefore wasn't a street, Gardener Crescent would have been more appropriate a name), where his very special friend was ready to be entertaining for him. The younger Dempsey male, unbeknownst to any of the other Dempseys had lied when he said he was going to work. At that very moment in time and space he was also to be found on a small, respectable cul-de-sac called, inappropriately, Gardener

Street. This was not a coincidence or a "Godincidence" nor fate or any such thing. This was curiosity. His dad was uncharacteristically cheery. Something unconscionable was afoot, Proctor could feel it in his fingernails, which tingled at the idea of investigating The Strange Case Of The Strangely Happy Father. The man was not attending Bible classes, that was for sure. Proctor Dempsey, tattooed conspicuously over his entire upper body, tried to look inconspicuous as he followed the jovial old man, one might almost call him a smug old man.

The problem with looking through keyholes is, you see things you don't want to see.

Chapter, the Eleventh
Schmental

The sun shone on the priests and the artists and the train drivers alike. The sun didn't care for the righteous above the wicked, it gave its equal brilliance equally. It was man's job to discriminate. Jessica Inmate had been discriminated against and saw the sun mostly through glass and iron. The sun had grown tardy while she was in jail. Why did it move so slowly? Was it becoming a geriatric? 'Go faster!' she yelled at the sky, ending with a sigh truncated by frustration. 'FASTER!'

'Dempsey, Dempsey, Dempsey!' The prison guard shouted until the woman realised she was getting called and responded to her name: no-one ever called her SmYth, or even Smith, on account of it not legally being her name, 'You have visitors.'

Jessica Unclean hadn't received guests since she was sent down. 'Oh me, oh my, who can that be? Do I have time to change? Is my hair okay? It's dirty, isn't it? Is it a man? Does he have a bum made of steel? Is he going to whisk me away? Oh my, mood: jubilant!'

Her status changed immediately to 'mood: crushed'. It was only her sister and the brats. Jessica Disappointed sat with them.

'Are you here to see me?' she asked, scanning the room for anyone with a better than average ass for their age and looks. Natalie Smyth, still single and still very much looking, ignored the mental question from her mental sister. The twins smiled at the mental question from their mental aunt, 'Who else would we be here to see?' they thought to each other in their faux-mindreading fashion, 'I know, right?' they both thought in reply.

'The twins look different,' Jessica Uninterested said. The twins had shared their 13th birthday during their aunt's incarceration and had decided amongst themselves that they were old enough to make their own decisions. Leah stopped letting her mum dye her hair brown and Luke stopped the bleaching routine of his hair. They also stopped wearing a long white dress and white wraparound top/beige trousers, respectively. In short, they had put an end to their mother's insistence that they look like Luke and Leia from Star Wars and looked like teenagers. Leia and Luke Smyth were not so short of their own psychological burdens that they also needed the bear their mother's.

'Goddamn teenagers, all they do is eat and complain,' their mother said.

The exclamation wasn't factually accurate. Whilst they did eat a great deal, as growing children are annoyingly prone to do on account of their developing bodies craving a constant supply of nutrients to replace those the body is tearing through, and they did partake in the occasional complaint to make their mother's face twitch (that was just for sport), they also did all manner of other things. They slept, they excreted waste, they watched TV, they played their PSPs, they got into nightclubs where their cousin Proctor worked as a bouncer, they drank alcohol, they smoked cigarettes, they helped cousin Proctor's boss deliver packages to the seniors at school and got paid for it, they became mini entrepreneurs taking mysterious packages for a fee and saving up almost enough money so far for an expensive slimline laptop that they could hide in a drawer. They never sampled the goods they delivered so it's not like Natalie Smyth – God, how I want a man! How wrong would it be to pay for one? – had to worry about her offspring becoming addicts then having to prostitute themselves out as a novelty twin pair. Just to be sure, she had arranged a visit to the prison under the guise of visiting their aunt, but the true purpose was to show them what happened when people get on the wrong side of the law, be it by downloading or prostituting themselves on the computer. It was too late, as the twins' own brand of heinous crime, in which they were currently engaged, was drug running for a local Godfather, owner of two nightclubs, a tanning salon, a used car dealership and a tea room. The tea room was an upmarket one that sold a roll and bacon for £7.95. The pig that the bacon came from was not reared on diamonds dipped in saffron, and the rolls were not made from manna and kneaded by virgins on Mount Olympus. They were rolls bought on the cheap and the same bacon you'd get at a burger van for 80p. But he charged five pennies short of eight quid. People paid it. His little tea room therefore made almost as much profit as his Ecstasy Empire. Evian is naïve spelled backwards. Still, only mole-people drank water from the tap.

The sun shone on the twins as they ferreted packages to school. It was good shit. The Local Godfather cared for the community and only sold second hand cars that his personal guarantee guaranteed would run for six months and his ecstasy was cut with only the finest sugar, with a little touch of salt. An elemental analysis of his drugs wouldn't show any cement powder or baby talc. He often fantasized about winning Local Citizen of the Year for his altruism. What a guy! Yet, whenever he went outside, it rained on him. Go figure.

'When do you think we can leave?' the twins thought to each other.

'This is so boring,' they replied telepathically (sort of).

'I know, right?' they moaned non verbally together.

Jessica Dempsey Wanna Be Smyth and Natalie Smyth Wanna Be Laid didn't speak to each other during the hour.

'Well, I think that should do it,' Natalie said after 59 minutes of silence, 'we'll be off.'

'Right. Bye,' Jessica said. Status: wtf is wrong with my mental sister?

They weren't close.

Chapter, the Twelfth
Suspicious Minds

Proctor had nowhere else to go. He left anyway with unclean eyes. He had seen a great many things in his violence-packed life, but what he saw when he looked through that letterbox on Gardener Street ... That's still not for now ... But the question about what Proctor Dempsey could do about it is. How do you wash unclean eyes? With copious amounts of water. Water has the cleaning ability of toast (buttered). Cillit Bang would give the eyes a proper clean, but there's the risk of long-term brain damage. And no eyes left. Cillit Bang would clean the eyes to nothingness. Sparkling, spit-shined, eat your dinner off it nothingness. The risk assessment says no to Cillit Bang. Cillit Bang says no to Cillit Bang in the eyes. Though he had nowhere else to go, Proctor Dempsey left anyway to stare directly at the sun. Veronica noticed he was gone. She didn't ask why. It was life as normal for the remaining inhabitants of the Dempsey Household. Regular routine was returned. The re-established regular morning routine with the bathroom was the most welcome, with Mr Dempsey having exclusive use between 0630 and 0715 and Veronica abluting (and so forth) between 0720 and 0745. Without Proctor's inconsiderate use of the bathroom 'whenever he had to pee' the home was already a much more routine one. This pleased Veronica greatly. Everything was more manageable with a regular bowel movement between 0720 and 0730, a shower between 0730 and 0737 and a good floss, brush and gargle taking Veronica up to 0744 and 50-odd seconds. Clicks, hisses and buzzes from colleagues were all so much easier on the colon when it had been emptied between 0720 and 0730.

Doc Savage monitored VD (Veronica Dempsey, not Venereal Disease, Vanilla Dogs, Vendredi Dimange, nor any other VD) with suspicion. The Doctor had hoped when she took on a backwards 'Beautiful Mind' type as a postgraduate student that the lab would be awash with sparks of genius. She expected to be showered in prestigious scientific publications and be an invited speaker at such acclaimed places as Durham. In her wildest fantasies she was accepting the Nobel Prize for Chemistry. Instead what she got was a student with piss poor NMRs and results that looked like she had sneezed into her reaction. But still. There was something going on with VD (not Valentine's Day!). Something to make Doc Savage eye her suspiciously. VD (not Velvet Dragons (that's a new one) or Violent Demise) had impeccable timing, never late and never took a minute longer for lunch than she should. But still! Something was going on. Something untoward. Something that Doc Savage couldn't quite finger.

VD was, as we know, stealing from the university to furnish her Loft Lab and supply her illegal opiate activity, but this information was not in the public domain. But still. If Doc Savage eyed VD (no, not Victor Delta) less and looked at her accounts more closely she would have caught on. But still. It was only a matter of time. Veronica's time was running out with Doc Savage. Veronica, who was usually hopeless at picking up on subtle signals from other people, found her primal instinct took over and alerted her to danger from the boss lady. She became suspicious of Doc Savage's sidelong glances and long gazes when she thought she couldn't be seen. Doc Savage, to her credit, sensed that VD (the Dempsey girl, not Vertical Drop) was sensing, in the first place, her own suspicion and it was mirrored back to her with some of

VD's amplifying it up. They reached a stalemate of suspicion. But still. There was more to this girl than she was letting on. But still.

Doc Savage may appear to those who only knew her for a few seconds to have got on in life by shouting at people till she got her own way. That was only true approximately (that's a scientific term) half the time. She did also have a sharp brain. Sums were never her thing or she may have caught on to the Loft Lab scam whilst looking over her accounts. Numerical ability left to the side, Doc Savage engaged her brain. Her sharp brain computed the problem and the variables. 'Hmm,' the brain said, pondering possibilities. The brain shortlisted the options: number one, ask her what she's up to; number two, sack the deviant; number three, hire a non-suspicious investigator, and, its personal favourite, number four, kill her and centrifuge her brain extracting the information directly as to what she's been up to. Doc Savage disengaged the brain and considered the shortlist: number one, dismissed, she might just lie therefore too risky; number two, what if she continued her PhD somewhere else and they got the Nobel Prize? That wasn't a chance she could take at all, oh no, idea dismissed; number three, interesting and intriguing, might just work, possible plan, and number four ... Well, it's thinking outside the box ... Does the technology exist to extract thoughts from dead matter? Probably not, therefore dismissed. Option three became Plan A. She hired a private investigator by the name D. Ville – which was assumed to be a fake name but was actually his christened at birth moniker. His teeth, which appeared at first and subsequent viewings to be fake, were also actually real. He paid an orthodontic specialist to file all his teeth into points, or 'fangs' as he thought of them. This was not done for religious or tribal reasons, not by frog licking nor a display of bravery, but by an orthodontic practitioner called Neville who wore a gleaming white coat (which stained under a UV light, not so clean as shaven), done under regular anaesthetic for aesthetic purposes only. Not a particularly inconspicuous mouth, but that's what happens when you hire people straight off the internet because they're cheap and you pay up front. He didn't bathe daily. He, instead, abluted with baby wipes, one per morning. The Mayans had pointy teeth, bathed daily and made blood sacrifices. He ate his steak medium-well. No matter, he wasn't paid to inconspicuously follow VD (Veronica – if you're up to something you're so going to get found out now! – Dempsey, not Voluptuous Dentals), but was placed in the lab in a technician's role, which was, in itself, a conspicuous move. As the age-old saying goes, 'three students do not a technician require'.

Davey Jones kicked things over and threw himself into his seat when he heard the news. What chance would his fantasies with the two girls have with this older man in the lab? Girls were always getting crushes on older men. Even, he presumed, ones with fangs. They may even find that a turn on. Certainly it would earn the newcomer points on the alpha male scale. Davey Jones thought he was alpha male in his circle, not unreasonably since was the solo male. He was, of course, wrong. Doc Savage was the alpha male, even with a fanged male in the vicinity.

D. Ville wasted no time in getting to know his subject. The crazy blond shouty woman was right; the girl was hiding something. It took him less than a day to discover the discrepancies in chemical orders and less than a week to conclude her loft should be investigated. He violated the loft (the loft knew it was going to happen and felt the violation no less violently because of the knowing) and discovered the equipment borrowedwithoutpermission from the university. He had no idea the magnitude of what he had discovered, and why should he, was he employed by the Nobel Prize Committee to discover who was inventing the equivalent of the wheel? Ah no, he was employed by the shouty woman to discover what was going on with the strange girl in the lab, the strangest girl in the lab. The loft held no large-scale meth lab or cannabis farm, he'd seen all that before. Just a couple of round-bottom flasks with a hypnotic mesmerising magenta potion and a smell that made him forget why he was there and masked the fact that this was the biggest find of his life.

Chapter, the Thirteenth
Showdown At The BS Corral

The portents were all in position. The moon remained resolutely in place after the sun had risen. The watery blue sky, almost white at the horizon, benefitted nothing from the extended and outstayed welcome of the moon. As Veronica stepped outside she was so surprised by the presence of the lesser celestial body she pointed at it and said, 'Oh, look at that, the moon,' to no one in particular, just as a black cat ran across her path. If God exists, whether you believe it or not makes no odds. If omens really are ominous they also supersede belief. Veronica Scientific Dempsey had no religious or magical inclinations. Pointing at the moon was just pointing at the moon. A black cat crossing her path was just a black cat going for a stroll in her vicinity. It being Friday the 13th meant it was the day after Thursday the 12th and the day before Saturday the 14th. That was all. Nothing more. To Veronica Scientific Dempsey, that was.

She got to the laboratory at 0859 precisely exactly as normal. There was a yellow post-it note at her workstation:

Come and see me when you get in,

BS

That was a bit unlucky, to get called in to a meeting with the boss. But the note had probably been there since the night before, so did it really have anything to do with Veronica's moon pointing, or the neighbour's wayward cat, or the date? BS, in this instance, standing for Barta Savage, and not the more common use of the BS initials meaning bullshit. "Come and see me when you get in, bullshit", was not the note.

Doc Savage's skin was furious and her eyes locked down on Veronica Dempsey, holding her in position for their showdown.

'What's going on?' was her opening gambit.

Veronica had been caught out by that trap before by answering in a literal, logical sense, but she as had nothing else to say she gave a literal and logical reply: 'You left a note for me to come in and see you.'

Doc Savage eyed her suspiciously. This girl was still her best hope at scientific fame, but she was fuming at the news brought to her by her private dick. The silence confused Veronica.

'The note was from you, wasn't it?' Veronica asked, 'Or was it bullshit after all?'

'What?'

'The note, BS, was it-'

'Nevermind that,' Doc Savage interrupted, her furious skin crackling. This girl was the most annoying creature she had ever had to deal with, but she was still her best – no, let's be truthful about it here – her *only hope* at a stratospheric career. 'It has come to my attention that you have been removing things from my laboratory and stealing chemicals which you have ordered and got me to sign for. You have been stealing, thieving. Stealing. That is unacceptable behaviour. Unacceptable behaviour. Do you have anything to say? I thought not. This is a case for instant dismissal. I need to know everything you have been doing and why.'

Veronica Dempsey was surprised by the revelation that her moonlighting was known to her boss. The rambling woman was still confusing her though. Of course it was something she should be sacked for, what other option was there? Why was the shouty woman not shouting and why did it not sound particularly like she was getting the sack? Veronica eyed Doc Savage suspiciously.

Doc Savage eyed Veronica suspiciously.

'What have you been doing at home, in your loft, with my chemicals? Your intellectual property belongs to me.'

That was true. Veronica had signed a contract. All her thoughts belonged to the university. All her discoveries belonged to the university. While she was *in* the university. Surely the loft was outwith the jurisdiction? Her Great Quest, Project Morphine Improvement, was initiated from one of the meetings of black people in her mind. Did the university own the intellectual property of the black people that held meetings inside her head? What would the loft say?

'If you don't tell me what you've been doing I'll get the police involved.'

'Police?'

'Ah good, you've heard of them,' the Doc's voice was becoming savage. 'I understand your mother is in prison.'

'Prison?'

Veronica Dempsey was in a pickle. She didn't want to have to talk to the police about what she did in the loft because they wouldn't understand. She didn't want to have to tell Doc Savage about what she did in the loft because she would understand.

'I'm not ready yet,' Veronica said.

'That's not good enough,' her boss said. It was good enough and her skin eased temporarily. The girl had more or less said she would give up all her information.

'I'm not ready yet,' Veronica said again.

'When then?'

'Next week.'

The terms were acceptable to Doc Savage. They were also acceptable to Veronica Is She A Genius? Dempsey. If the morphine was good shit then Veronica would need an accomplice. Doc Savage would do fine. She would probably have told her anyway, without all this big song and dance about it.

There was only one way to find out of the opiate, made from magenta solutions, was good shit. Veronica Dempsey, never smoked, never drank alcohol, never took drugs, never looked at porn, never been kissed, never tortured an animal, went home at 1800 hours, went to the loft, took some barely pink powder from the drying oven, measured 10 mgs on the microscales, dissolved it in Evian (after all, she was not a mole-person) and drank it.

Chapter, the Somethingth Magenta Morphean Delight

'Jupiter-pah-dupider. Bouncing belly beach balls (tee hee). Caramel. Creamy smooth caramely caramel with chunks of caramel and caramel. Tuesday. Friday. Tuefriday. Bendopat. Mamma mia, here I go again. Enter night. Take my hand. We're off to NeverDisneyLand. Cat poop surprise. Zero. Hero. No time flat. Zero. Hero. Just. Like. That. Laces: strawberry, leather, yellow. I need to give away my laces. Please take my laces. You need laces? Got good laces. Get your laces here! Laces? Lace. Not lace, to lace. I want a viscount! 71% of 16 women agreed. Take my hand. Dizzy now. Time? Tuefriday the umpteth a la seventyteen. Floor. Ceiling. Floling. Oiling. QUIET! Christ's disciples went that way. Christ's disciples went to play. Hide and seek. Peek! I SAID QUIET! Brain, make sense. Brain whereforeartthou? Brain, I love you. I love your cauliflower passages. Heilbron McGyver renders your argument invalid. You're the most beautiful brain in the world and I love you more than … Whaddya wanna make those eyes at me for? Front, quarter, upper, quarter, right, quarter, upper anticlockwise, quarter, right anticlockwise, quarter, front anticlockwise, quarter. Meh. Noise, ack! Dad's home. Shh. Sleep. Shhhh. Wikipedia noise.'

'Veronica?'

It wasn't dad's voice.

'She's not home,' Veronica called from the loft. That would fix it. She lay on the floor with her eyes closed and muttered through a smile.

'Where was I? I love you brain. Brainy brain of food, brain. A roll and brain. Brain on rye. Brain soup. Brain toastie with pepper. God in heaven, Amen. Warm heat. Quietly now. I SAID QUIETLY NOW! Mouse, quietly now, like you know. Dizzy. Century blood. Tiny little paisley pattern baldness like worms on a plate.'

'Veronica?' The voice that wasn't dad's called again.

'Not here!' She called back. She scratched her nose, it was very itchy. She opened her eyes. The loft was dark. She wondered when it got late. She wasn't ready to move yet.

'Veronica?' The voice sounded like it was in the room with her, but it wasn't a voice she knew.

'Veronica's not he-' Eli and Samuel and God. Why she suddenly remembered the story at that point is a mystery. Her brain was not functioning in its normal, rational manner. Nonetheless, the story came to mind and she stopped trying to say she wasn't home and, instead, called out, 'Is that you, God[5]?'

The voice didn't answer, which Veronica Stoned Out Her Nut Dempsey took to be definitive proof that it was God that had spoken. Her mutterings quietened. Her breathing slowed and just as she drifted off into a deep, soothing sleep she thought, 'Well, that was interesting.'

---

[5] See The Bible, 1 Samuel chapter 3 verses 2-10 for the story. The abridged version is that Samuel is asleep and hears his name called. He goes to Eli and says, 'sup?', but Eli tells him he didn't call him. This happens a couple of times – both losing sleep every time – and eventually they wonder if it's God that's calling Samuel. Turns out it was. Read from verse 11 onwards to find out what He wanted.

Chapter, the Fifteenth
Plan A

The prodigal brother, disappeared for ten years then resurfaced the same day Veronica began her second degree, then left again three weeks previously having followed his father on one of his Gardener Street Excursions and looked through the letterbox (shocking his brain all the way back to the late 18th century), had returned to the family home late in the evening of Friday the 13th. What did he have to be superstitious about? Superstitions were for pussies and girls. He knew his dad had gone to Gardener Street again so he came to see Veronica while his dad was otherwise engaged. The door wasn't locked but he had a key anyway. Veronica wasn't in the lounge or the kitchen. He called out to her. There was a reply from … was it the loft? What was it with the females in his family and the loft? He went upstairs; she wasn't in her bedroom or the bathroom. He called again. The reply was definitely from the loft. Up he went. His sister lay on the carpet, mumbling and smiling, laughing and shaking her head. He said her name. She asked if he was God. He sat on the floor and watched her. He didn't know why the loft looked like a high school chemistry lab, but he'd seen enough junkies to know that she was on something. She was wearing her jacket.

'What have you done?' He said, softly.

'God knows,' she replied.

'God doesn't exist,' he said.

'Shut up, I'm talking to Him, aren't I? Go go gadget tentacles!'

He moved to beside her head and stroked her hair till her mutterings quietened, and her breathing slowed. Just as she drifted off into a deep, soothing sleep she said, 'Well, that was interesting.'

She woke up lonely.

It worked. Did it work? What worked? It did. But did it? It did. What did it do? It did it. How did it work? Chemistry. Why did it work? Magic. It did work though, eh? It worked. Did it work? How? Chemistry. Why? Magic. Because. And then. Ha! It worked! Stone me! They might. It worked. It did. It did. It did. Veronica smiled with teeth. It worked. Probably. One data set does not a conclusion make. Not a scientific one. She couldn't use herself again, that would defeat the purpose. By God, it worked.

Veronica squared up to her moment of Fate. The meeting of black people in her brain was adjourned for the festival of Ranavandoonaditch. No help there. She could ask her dad. Oh, the humour! Where did that come from? Ha ha ha. Ask dad. Good one. Veronica had to go solo on this. She considered herself lucky. So few people realise when their Moment is and miss it. One would think when Fate went to all the bother to set up a Moment it would call ahead and let people know. Was Fate lazy? Or just didn't have a good staff? Missed Moments with Fate was mankind's biggest woe. Woe is me! Woe are we! Who are you? Fate. Good to meet you, what have you got in store for me? Wouldn't you like to know?

Everyone gets a Moment. People who respond well sometimes get two. Rarely more than that are given to any one person. People don't make their own Fate. People may try and make their own fate. Those are people that have recognised their Moment anyway. This was Veronica – 22 years old, average weight, average height, average brown hair, average brown eyes, average top speed, average bowel movements, above average recall, less than average social intellect – Dempsey's Moment. Her First Moment. Fate had another in store. What would she do? What were her options? She could do nothing with her barely pink, made from glorious magenta solutions, powder. Pretend she had never made it. Bin it, ditch it, flush it, burn it, decompose it, send it to hell in a handbasket: from atoms it came, to atoms it shall return according to the Grand Conservation of Matter, so say we all. It was an option. What else? She could sell it on the black market. It was an option, but it was too illegal with too much wondering if the fuzz were onto her, always worried, always nervous, always making mistakes, always on the lamb-chop. What else? Go public, legit. Tell the world. Heal the world. Let the world decide if it worked, properly, truly worked. It wouldn't be without its share of worry, nerves and making mistakes, but it wasn't illegal. Well, it wouldn't be illegal as soon as she 'fessed up to Doc Savage and got her on board.

She faced up to her Moment. The easy option was to burn it, burn everything. The fire could eat her genius. She knew she could achieve it, it worked. That was enough, wasn't it? Veronica Dempsey Did It! Veronica Dempsey didn't really care about other people's opinions, why should anyone else need to know that she did it? Would it alter her discovery if more people knew? No. Option one it is then. She would give Doc Savage a cock and bull story about her loft activity. Sorted.

Fate coughed conspicuously. The loft waited.

But.

Fate sighed, the loft exhaled.

Okay, but.

She remembered the feeling. She smiled with teeth. She thought about adverts on television with sad people, sore people, pathetic people, dying people. She could help them, to varying extents, obviously.

Fate smiled on her, the loft puffed with pride. There she goes.

She couldn't help them all through the illegal option, too much worry and attention from the fuzz. Fine, option three then. Proper and legit. Doc Savage would be told first thing on Monday morning. Veronica Dempsey, average in almost every way and who underestimated on almost every level what her Loft Lab Discovery could do for mankind and the likes, toddled downstairs, poured herself Sugar Puffs, barely wetted with milk, topped with extra sugar, ate it in a regular fashion with the same proportions on every spoonful of milk, sugar, Sugar Puff puffs – ratio was everything – and then toddled back to her bedroom and drew up some acetates for presenting her findings to Doc Savage at 0901 on Monday morning. She drew out the long and laborious preparative pathway to her particular brand of opiate, keeping her sidechain secret ingredient a secret by calling it X.

God, it worked! Why wasn't the wheel invented before it was invented? She looked at it all written down in coloured pens on clear acetate; cycles, circles, pentagons, hexagons, secret chemistry codes, abbreviations and, most importantly, arrows, arrows and curly arrows: arrows right, left, backwards, sideways, swooping, short, cheeky, hopeful, "best guesses", double headed and fish hooks. She smiled with teeth.

Chapter, the Sixteenth
Previously, in Magenta Opium

In the story so far milk was spilled, cops left empty handed and growling. Cops returned and left with boxes of illegalness and a found mother, they smiled inwardly since it would be unprofessional to smile outwardly. They didn't say, 'you're nicked, sunshine'. Illegal mother went to jail and unrepentantly tried to perform an illegal act in the Big House because she's just not that smart. Alas, she was also not all that happy. Being not very smart is acceptable if you're happy. Happy trumps smart every time. She was neither. In her favour, she was delusional. Two big thumbs up on that.

The illegal jailbird was mother to a son with violent tendencies and a recently tattooed upperbody (including sleeves) who had also been a jaildude for a while on a couple of occasions. She was also mother to a girl. This girl was set to change the world, as such should probably be recapped last.

Basic biology dictates that where there are children there would, at some point anyway, be a man-slash-sperm donor. Said man-slash-sperm donor was still on the scene and lived pretty quietly while his wife was lost on purpose in the loft. He had sex with his wife precisely twice. She got pregnant both times. He had magnificent sperm. Sperm that lived for weeks and never gave up till they had fulfilled the biological imperative of fusing with an egg. If there were awards for sperm his would get Oscars, Nobel Prizes, Ryder Cups and be in the Guinness Book of World Records at the very least. His wife, pregnant both times she had sex, hated his super sperm and ceased all contact after her first child. A drunken debauched night a decade later resulted in the daughter and she double ceased all contact. He thought it was probably for the best, there was no telling what his sperm would do next. Truth be told, they wouldn't do much more than form a gamete, it's not like they were an evil genius bent on taking over the planet. Or were they? The husband had found comfort in the bosom of another woman, but details are sketchy at present, save to say she had a property on Gardener Street (which was a cul-de-sac, of all things!) and a tattoo of a butterfly stylised like a tribal insignia across her collarbone.

The sex-starved (by choice) inmate had a sex-starved (by not being able to convince anyone to shag her) sister. The sister also had two children, but as they were twins it cannot be said with any scientific certainty that the woman has had sex more than once in her life. The sister (sex-starved by circumstance rather than design) thought about sex so much she often wondered if she was really a man. She thought about having sex with men she saw at Burger King and didn't even fancy but might like the curl of their lip or the movement of their Adam's apple and she'd wet her pants. To date she had considered paying a man to shag her. She was just about to have a better idea.

The twins, niece and nephew to the banged-up woman and cousin to the girl about to change the world (in a manner of speaking, that is to say, to a certain extent), had lived in the shadow of their mother's Star Wars addiction for long enough and had recently found the strength to tell her 'no, we're not going to dress like retards any more,' and put a stop to the constant forced dressing up like Luke and Leia. Luke and Leia (the Star Wars twins) were siblings who snogged each other – where was their clairvoyance on that one? They also ran drugs for the local crime boss (not the Star Wars twins, the other twins), but that was just for pin money, and they were forced to do it because their mother thought computers were Satan's direct networking point to mankind and refused to hear any word on the subject of her buying one. The twins liked to eat and grew out of spite towards their mother.

The cleaners had been at it again, that much is certain. The "it" is more woolly. This "it" is not the "it" of having bacon rolls for breakfast on a Friday morning. They were at it as well, always, but the Holy Spirit does not lose sleep over bacon rolls every Friday morning. Monday to Thursday they ate toast which smelled like more toast. God Himself sanctions that "it". Not Father, Son nor Holy Spirit sanctions the "it" they've been at again.

To the point, the daughter of the inmate, the cousin of the Star Wars twins, sister to the tattooed bouncer, daughter of the oft content and oft smelly Gardner Street (oh, the nerve of the naming system!) visitor, the average of the average, the girl in the middle of the bell curve, the girl who had never been kissed and never even gave it a thought, was poised on a great scientific discovery. Unaware of the social and political repercussions it would cause, she had decided to share her discovery with the world, but first with her boss. She had coaxed reluctant rings to close with soft words and hard metals, she had eased out stereochemistry with a firm hand and bulky bases. All in her spare time, in between eating sandwiches and working for a shouting boss lady and along side a teeth-bleached girl and pent-up boy, under the scrutiny of a pointy fanged private investigator.

And now, the continuation.

Chapter, the Seventeenth
Conversation With The Dead, Part I

He was in the loft again. Not God, no. But yes God. Of course God. But not God. He must have been there before. He must probably have been there before. Probably. Maybe. He was there now, sitting, twitching, waiting to die. All alone, apart from God. And Veronica. Veronica watched him sit and twitch and die. Mr D. Ville, real name D. Ville, returned to the Loft Lab, which was uncharacteristic of him to begin with. He had an urge, deep in his veins, throbbing, urging him to return. His electrons wouldn't settle until he made up his mind to go back. The next uncharacteristic thing he felt compelled to do was eat the pink powder. He knew it wasn't clever to eat anything lying around a laboratory, clandestine or legitimate, but he felt like he would suffocate if he didn't taste the pretty baby pink powder. He had stared at it a long time. He looked at the door, his exit from the loft. He stared at the pink powder. The exit. The powder. Exit? Powder? It looked like strawberry sherbet (the powder, not the exit. The exit looked like a door). He dabbed a few grains on his tongue. It tasted like the inside of medicine, but he ate it. He looked towards the exit again. Electrons hurt in his brain. The loft remained quiet. The loft didn't want the man to die there, but the loft had no say in it: the less decisions that separated a man from death, the more likely he is to choose death. Mr D. Ville couldn't resist the baby pink allure that drew him towards oblivion. Only one decision and death was his. He had never thought about killing himself before, but there were too many steps involved. Not today. Today it was in his hands. He needed more powder. Two mouthfuls, crunched and swallowed. The last uncharacteristic thing he was going to do was die. In a stranger's loft, while she watched. It wasn't how he expected to go. He wanted to die during a spectacular gunfight in a strip club.

She couldn't stop him from dying; by the time she went up to the loft he had already eaten a deathly amount of the drug.

'What did you do?' she asked.

He looked sheepishly at her, pink powder still staining his pointy teeth.

'Why did you do that?' she asked.

He shrugged and looked even more sheepish. His mouth frothed.

'You're going to die,' she told him and sat down on the floor opposite him.

He nodded in a sheepish fashion. His frothing mouth foamed.

'Can't you go somewhere else?' she asked. What would she do with the dead body of a grown man?

'I'm sleepish,' he frothed, sheepishly. 'The cleaners, they're at it.'

He fell asleep, mumbling occasionally ('the cleaners, they're at it!' and 'mmm, strippers' for instance) and at some point he stopped breathing. Veronica kept breathing in and out. While he died she tried to think of how best to dispose of him. She couldn't report a dead body in her loft or the fuzz would take her to prison just like they did her mother. The loft had previous, that's never good. She could put him in the neighbour's bin. No, she couldn't, the council had become overly fussy about rubbish going in the correct receptacle – they didn't take the paper bin if it had plastic, they didn't take the garden bin if the logs were too big and they didn't take the wrong kind of can in the can recycling, they were hardly likely to lift a cadaver: Health and Safety rules were really getting to be a bore. Although it should probably be okay in the garden bin on account of the body decomposing, but she'd have to phone and check. After a minute thinking about it she decided she shouldn't phone the council and ask what bin to put a dead body in. There was only one other option she could think of.

Veronica Dempsey, not shy just generally uninterested, spoke to the ex-being lying on her loft floor for almost an hour, surpassing the total of all conversations she had exchanged with the living. She told him, or was 'it' now the technical term?, about the pink powder he-it had ate and about how she made it. It really did look like strawberry sherbet, was that a design flaw? Not her fault anyway. Atoms are as atoms do. She told he-it that one day she would like to have sex. That statement took her by surprise, even more so when she expanded on it by saying she wanted it to be tender and not just for procreation. The toluene fumes had a lot to answer for. She told the he-it-vessel that she'd never orgasmed ('why are you talking about all this?!'), but could appreciate the chemistry of the brain, she understood the chemistry of the brain when it happened, at the point of orgasm when the brain is flooded with charged, excited atoms, making nothing else in the world matter as a blanket of ecstasy wrapped itself all around. So she understood, anyway. Atoms are as atoms do. She tried to think herself an orgasm but it didn't work.

'Will you be okay?' she asked the empty body. 'I'm going to Tesco; it's all right, it's open 24 hours.'

The body didn't reply. Veronica Dempsey had, that morning, come clean to her academic supervisor about the chemicals she had taken and what she had tried to do with them – it did work, didn't it? – and had been absolved. For a grand total of 14 hours she had given up her status of Veronica The Fugitive. The magenta derived opium would be brought on as an official, but still secret, project. The loft, obviously sent to try, had managed to drag her under as a fugitive once again, like her mother before her. The loft objects! The loft didn't ask to be invaded by a pirating mother or clandestine daughter and most certainly not a sharp-toothed private dick with a death wish! The loft claims to not be a party to the events! The loft wants its 'previous' stricken! The jury is hung. The loft was currently the coffin to a snooping now-deceased investigator. Veronica Dempsey, for a total of 14 hours, managed to be Veronica The Non-Fugitive, but her grace time was up. She, once again, slipped into the familiar, well-fitting skin of Veronica The Fugitive as she put into action Operation Get Rid Of The Dead Body. Tesco was her first stop. Proctor was her second.

Chapter, the Eighteenth
Conversation Over The Dead

'Eh, no,' Proctor said when he saw the dead body on the floor of the loft, 'this isn't a "small favour".'

Veronica shrugged, 'It's not like I asked you to kill him.'

'True,' he replied, 'but this is the next worse thing!'

'What about rape?' she asked.

'What about rape?' he asked back.

'What about rape?' she asked again, not understanding his confusion.

'What about rape?' he asked again too.

'Raping someone is worse than carrying a dead body about,' she explained.

'What?'

'Me asking for help lifting a body is not "the next worse thing" to me asking you to kill someone, for instance, rape.'

'Right,' he said, 'and all those years away from you all I thought I was the crazy one of the family. I'm the fourth craziest.'

He looked at the lifeless body again, it was still as dead as nature dictated it would be. He looked at his little sister. She was breathing. Did she have homicidal tendencies? He looked at the still dead body once again.

'What did you do?' he asked.

'It wasn't me,' she said. Was he accusing her? Did she care? She certainly wasn't offended by the accusation.

'Did Dad?' he had a flashback to the Gardener Street Incident, 'He's not a killer, is he?'

'Not dad.'

'So this stranger crawled into our loft to die?' he asked.

'Yes,' Veronica replied, 'although he probably walked in. Are you going to help me or not?'

'Of course,' he said kindly, 'but I've never had to deal with a dead body, I'm not sure what to do. Should we put it in the neighbour's bin?'

Veronica shook her head sagely, 'No, the council.'

'Yeah, fair enough,' he nodded.

'I know what to do with Mr Ville,' she said, 'I'm just not physically strong enough. And I don't have a car.'

'Mr Ville?' Proctor shouted.

'Do you know him?' Veronica asked.

'No, but you do?'

'Yes,' she said, 'is it important?'

'I thought he was just a randomer,' he said, 'but you know him?'

'He's worked at uni for the last few weeks,' she explained.

'Doing what?'

'Spying mainly, I should think.'

'On you?' he asked.

'On this,' Veronica motioned to the Loft Lab contents.

'Which brings me onto my next question,' he said, 'what the fuck is all this?'

'Just stuff,' she said.

'Stuff? Illegal stuff?'

'Not any more,' she answered, 'Now, this body's not getting any more flexible, can we make a start?'

'You have a plan, little genius sister?'

'I do, and you mean genius little sister,' she said.

'What if I mean you're a little genius?' he asked.

'Touché!' she said.
'Is it genius?'
'It'll do.'
'It'll do?'
'It'll do. Enough is as good as a feast.'

There are only a certain number of things you will do in your life; a certain number of places you will visit, a certain number of houses you will live in, a certain number of songs you will hear, a certain number of meals you will eat, a certain number of people you will insult, a certain number of words spoken … There will always be places unvisited, houses uninhabited, songs unsung to you, foods untasted, people unknown and words without the volume of utterance. Every word she used explaining to Proctor was one less word she could use for anything else and took her closer to her death. Death knows how many words you're allowed. Once the tally is up, you're his.

'It'll do? Enough is as good as a feast?'

'Are you okay?' She needed his strength, his car and his ability to not go running to the fuzz about this, but she had her doubts about his overall sanity.

'Are you okay?' he asked.

'Please stop repeating me, what are you, thirteen years old again? I am okay. You will be okay. Maybe if I had more time to think about it I might manage a better plan, but right now it's the plan. It's the only plan, so it's the plan.'

'Okay, I trust you,' Proctor said, 'what do we do?'

'I've been to Tesco, but can you take me to Asda and Morrisons? I can't walk to them and I don't want to get the bus at this time of night.' Too many words! Veronica Dempsey wondered if texting counted towards the Death Tally.

Until that point Veronica hadn't given any thought to the purpose of having a big brother, but she could see now it had advantages. He was physically stronger than she was and he was probably quite good at driving by now, since he'd been doing it on and off since he was old enough to have sex, which he carried out with much the same frequency, to be specific, when he was not in jail. Good driving would be important, she wouldn't want to draw attention to them on the trip to the West Country.

'We're going *where*?' Proctor asked.

'West Country,' she repeated.

He put the body of the person that was Mr D. Ville, private investigator with no self-control, in a big suitcase. It fitted, after a fashion, and he put the suitcase in the boot of his orange VW Polo. The Polo was red once, but the paint job hadn't stood up well to the weather and the car could only truthfully be described as orange by anyone who didn't know it was once red; by those who knew its original colour it could be described as very pale red going towards orange rather than pink. The suitcase was black with a rainbow strap. It was a smooth and normal transaction.

Veronica and Proctor walked around Asda in a smooth and normal fashion, pretending to be on a smooth and normal shopping excursion, buying a pack of sausage rolls from the fridge, a two litre bottle of coke from the juice aisle, a loaf of bread from the bread aisle, an 18 pack of assorted flavour crisps from the snack aisle, a variety pack of Cadbury's from the sweet aisle and a jumbo box of detergent from the cleaning aisle. In what looked like a spontaneous purchase, Veronica put a rolling pin (from the home-ware aisle) in the small trolley just before getting to the checkout. Nobody in Asda looked at them as if they had recently stuffed a suitcase with a deceased private investigator and they managed to pay for their goods without accidentally mentioning it to the cashier. They did the same in Morrisons, wandering around, pretending to not have a dead body in the boot of their car (which they were getting very good at and had pretty much perfected the walk of a person not up to the eyeballs in dead person trouble), but in Morrisons they didn't buy a rolling pin and they bought a five pack of Double Deckers from the sweet aisle in place of the variety pack of chocolate. Veronica paid cash. On the back seat of the once red Polo were green and white Asda, blue and white Tesco and yellow and white Morrisons bags. In the boot the former Mr D. Ville was quietly decomposing into the black suitcase tied in a rainbow ribbon. In the front seats Proctor and Veronica played I Spy.

Chapter, the Nineteenth
Concurrent Events

In the late evening of Monday the 16th Veronica Dempsey, initials VD, killed and didn't kill D. Ville, initials DV. Philosophically speaking she killed him. She made the pink powder that he ate; had she not made the pink powder that he ate then he couldn't have ate it (since it wouldn't exist) and he wouldn't have died in her loft. Philosophically speaking, she didn't kill him; he ate it of his own free will and if he was the sort of person to go about eating mysterious substances that he found lying about laboratories from indeterminate and suspicious sources then he wasn't long for this world anyway. Philosophically speaking she killed him and she didn't kill him. He was like Schrödinger's cat, the most famous of all hypothetical cats that is both dead and alive at the same time, apparently allegedly. Dead and alive. Killed by and not killed by her. The problem with theoretical physics and philosophy is that the cat will always die (it's not an immortal) and Mr D. Ville is, and always will be, henceforth, dead. Try this on for size: all protons are sub-atomic particles, but not all sub-atomic particles are protons. She killed him and didn't kill him simultaneously and forever.

*

In the late evening of Monday the 16th Proctor Dempsey was parked on Gardener Street with unclean eyes. The engine was off and he sat in silence. The heating was off and he sat in the growing cold. He didn't want to be there. Not really. He didn't want to know how often his dad visited her. Not really. But it was three times a week, an hour and a half per "session". He knew. He didn't want to know how many other people visited her regularly. Not really. Four visits per night, average. 9 males per 1 female, average. He knew. He most certainly didn't want to wait till his dad left and march up to her door and beg to be seen by her. Really. His dad left. Proctor waited in the silence and the ever-creeping coldness till his dad was gone before he got out the car. There would be a 30-minute hiatus between her visitors which should be enough time to arrange something with her, if she was likely to be amicable to the idea of receiving his propositions. Something he didn't want to do, but absolutely had to do. Really. Even if he just looked at her properly. He had been there every evening, watching from a distance. When he was at work his spirit was still in Gardener Street, watching over her and her companions. He hadn't been able to stop thinking about her, and his brain was grated to tiny shreds during every moment of it because he could only picture her with his dad and he most certainly didn't want to think about that image. Ever. He needed to be able to think about her freely. He had to get an image of her away from his dad before he had no functioning brain left. He reached her gate. He opened her gate. Was that a yell from inside the house? He reached out for her doorbell. His phone rang. Veronica. Odd. She never used the phone, she didn't even text. Three days ago he would have bet his life that she didn't take drugs either. Something was going on. The mystery of his geeky sister overtook the mysterious woman whose door he currently darkened and he drew his hand back from the bell and answered his phone.

'Hey, wassup?'

'It's Veronica,' she said unnecessarily, 'Can you do me a small favour?'

*

In the late evening of Monday the 16th the woman with the tribal butterfly tattooed on her upper chest said goodbye to Mr Dempsey. He was one of her favourites. They were all one of her favourites, but he was one of her favourites. She went back upstairs and looked out the window. He was there again. The man with the sleeves, the man with the young face but hard eyes. He was a Dempsey, she was sure of it. It was one of her gifts, being able to see familial resemblance in things other than appearance. The longer he took to approach the house the more she wanted him to. The more pathetic they seemed the stronger they performed. And besides, she quite fancied seeing the rest of his ink. It didn't look like particularly good work, he'd probably only paid a few hundred for work worth thousands, but no matter what he paid, he had to bleed through it and she wanted to see what he had done to himself that was worth all the pain. She watched with pleasure as he got out his car. He got to the gate. He opened the gate. She braced herself and slammed her loose arm back into its socket. Dislocated shoulders were an occupational hazard. The only thing better than dislocating it was relocating it back in position; she delayed the sensation as long as she could. She looked outside again, he was going for the doorbell. He was stopping. He was answering his phone. He was walking away. She was disappointed. And she realised she was wrong. Seeing him more closely was enough to know he would never be a client. He may be considered pathetic for many things, but not in the way she needed.

*

In the late evening of Monday the 16th, Natalie – sex, sex, please sex, anyone – Smyth was looking at the Escort section of the Yellow Pages. Not the Ford Focus precursor Escort, the male kind of escort where you pay a man for company and if you get the right company he will sex you. But how to know what company to use. Was there a code? Do they all do the sex thing? How do you ask? She closed the Yellow Pages, it was too complicated. All she wanted was sex. ALL she wanted was sex. Sex please, anyone? Please? Anyone? She didn't even mind if money changed hands. And then it hit her, just-like-that. Money can change hands, but why should it go from hers to his? She could get paid for sex. Ironically, although she couldn't encourage a single male to sleep with her for free, when she decided to charge for it an orderly queue formed.

*

In the late evening of Monday the 16th the Wrong Order Twins had a spiffing idea! 'Let's learn Kung Fu!' they thought at precisely the same time as each other. 'Okay!' they replied.

*

In the late evening of Monday the 16th Jessica, once Smyth, now Dempsey, never Rabbit, slept in her prison cell. Her sleep was boring and empty; she never dreamed.

*

In the late evening of Monday the 16th Doc Savage poured herself another large glass of Merlot and poured over her computer. She was scripting her acceptance speech for her Nobel Prize. She had been working on it for years and now she could fill in the blanks – the thieving little bitch Veronica was going to win her it after all. Merlot was delicious. Merlot was her teeth's best friend because it turned them an interesting shade of greypurple that they liked being. Far more interesting than having white or yellow teeth. Greypurple toothed people made good dinner party guests, she thought. She stood up and clutched her Merlot glass to her bosom like a trophy and began speaking:

'I'd like to thank the committee for this wonderful award. Many people ask where I get my Nobel Prize winning ideas and all I can say is, I'm gifted. My brain is as toned as Peter Andre's stomach ... back when he sang that song in a swimming pool. I don't know what it's like now. The good thing about my brain is it's still in tiptop condition, it's toned and rippling. But seriously,' she sipped and gulped through greypurple teeth, 'I'm thrilled that my little molecule, the Wonder Drug if you want to call it that, has had such a positive effect on the world. When I first thought about how I could make a drug like this, morphine only better, if you will, I could only dream it would achieve this.' She bowed to her imaginary audience and summed up with her killer line, 'God himself may have invented opium, but I perfected it.'

People have killed for less.

*

In the late evening of Monday the 16th Davey Jones took his cat for a walk in a harness. Meanwhilst Pauline Burns emailed famous people and asked if they could be friends. The cleaners were dreaming about being at it again.

*

In the late evening of Monday the 16th D. Ville, initials DV, was and was not killed by Veronica Dempsey, initials VD, without a gunshot in earshot or a tits out female stripper in sight.

Chapter, the Twentieth
Road Trip

In the late late evening of Monday the 16th VD, her brother PD and a deceased DV headed west; PD driving, VD passenging and DV seeping essential fluids and bodily elements into the black polymer fibres of his suitcase coffin. Proctor ate a sausage roll and said, 'I spy with my little eye something beginning with SR.' Veronica guessed Sausage Road – no, he told her – Skanky Rose – no – Shaky Roll – no – Starry Rise – no – September Rain – no, it's August – Sandy Remember – no, are you getting bored? What sort of guess is that? – Sausage Roll! – no – Segmented Road – no, but close – Sandwiched Road – no – Segmented Roll – no – Squirrel Roadkill – no – I give up. The answer was Shiny Road. He would have accepted Sparkly Road, but not Segmented or Sandwiched Road. Veronica ate a Double Decker. 'I spy with my little eye,' Proctor said again, 'something beginning with DD.' Veronica guessed Dempsey Dempsey – no – Dark Drive – no – Door Dimple – no – Double Dempsey – no – Double Dare – no – December Diet – no. After five minutes of guessing she gave up. The answer was Double Decker.

They drove for a while in silence and Veronica dozed. Proctor thought about the Tattooed Woman Of Gardener Street and how close he came to ringing her bell. He imagined that his sister hadn't phoned at the most inopportune moment to have him aid and abet her in the disposal of a body and he imagined instead that his finger made contact with the plastic, he imagined pressing it in, he imagined a chime on the other side and he imagined seeing her figure sashay down the hall. He imagined her answering the door in a black lace transparent dressing gown and he didn't have to imagine his hard-on. He couldn't imagine any further while he was driving so he went back to the beginning and he imagined that his sister hadn't interrupted as he was about to ring the doorbell. He imagined from Veronica not phoning through imagined actual doorbell pressing to negligeed woman approaching and opening the door on a loop as he drove through Mordor, past Brigadoon, over the Styx, skimming by Atlantis on the left, the Islets of Langerhans on the right and arrived at their destination beyond the Seven Seas of Rhye in the shadow of a moon-rainbow in Devonshire.

When Veronica first left the newly deceased private dick to decompose in her loft and visited Tesco she used their computer section to hire a cottage with no near neighbours and a steel bathtub and, most importantly, that was currently empty. Every little helps. She had no romantic notion about where she would take a body for disposal. The Lakes would have been an incredibly scenic place, with rolling hills and clear, expanses of reflective water; tranquil to the max. To get rid of a body is a dastardly thing to do, but that doesn't mean one has to be a heathen about it. But as she had no compunction to see any of the sights she took the most suitable she could find in a hurry. As Veronica Mad Scientist Dempsey had killed and not killed the Snooping Investigator, getting rid of the body was both a dastardly and a not dastardly thing to do. On the whole, it was dastardly. They arrived at their destination and the dastardly plot was put into full operation. Proctor, Ex-Con and all round Handy Man to have in a dead body crisis, broke into the cottage that Veronica hired, knowing, of course it would be empty as she had hired it from the morrow. On account of it being after midnight it was technically hardly illegal at all.

On account of the dead body in the boot it was insignificantly illegal altogether.

Veronica ran a warm bath – 'Is this really the time for it?' Proctor asked – and tipped in box after box after box of high enzyme action washing powder she had bought inconspicuously and paid cash for at Tesco, Asda and Morrisons. The bathtub frothed and bubbled and splurted soap and Mr D. Ville was sploshed into his watery grave, his penultimate resting place.

'Should we say a few words?' Proctor asked.

'I hope this works,' Veronica said stoically and they left, skimming past the Seven Seas of Rhye, the Islets of Langerhans on the left, Atlantis on the right, back over the Styx, past Brigadoon, back through Mordor and home.

Chapter, the TwentyFirst
The Promotion

The Wrong Order Twins invested the money they had been saving for a slimline laptop computer (slimline in order for it to be stored in a drawer without their mother's knowledge since mother objected in the strongest terms to goddamn kids having goddamn computers) into an intense martial arts training programme. It turned out they didn't actually need a computer now anyway as their benevolent Drug Overlord Boss had bought them both Blackberrys as a thank you for their sterling work in their (off the record) delivering of brown paper packages tied up with string to fellow school children, which is a euphemistic way of saying they delivered his drugs, which neither he nor they would ever say aloud. The Blackberrys were mini computers in their hand with internet access and Microsoft packages. They told their mum it was just a phone. They received calls on them, so how could she argue? Besides, she didn't have to buy them. Goddamn expensive technology of The Devil. Their sterling (on the record) activity in the benevolent Drug Overlord Boss's tea room hadn't gone unnoticed either and they were allowed as many cans of branded soda as they wanted over-and-above the usual part-time working allowance of a free plate of soup at lunch time.

They trained fast and they trained hard. Primarily they followed the disciplines of Kung Fu and Parkour. Kung Fu in order to think to each other, 'I know Kung Fu,' and reply in kind, 'Show me[6]', and Parkour because it was fucking cool[7]. They did press-ups, sit-ups, stomach crunches, upside down stomach crunches, jumping jacks, lifted weights, squatted with weights, ran with weights, stretches, and more press-ups and sit-ups etc and so forth. They did cardio, they toned and they increased strength and agility. Their clairvoyant ability was put to good use and they became a one-man fighting machine in two bodies, one male, one female; they fought with one mind and four elbows and knees.

Word of their exceptional physical efforts reached their Overlord Drug Boss and he was pleased. He always knew there was something special about those kids and he considered them fondly as the multiple birth children he never had. The Blackberrys and all-you-can-drink branded soda was no longer sufficient thanks in

---

[6] If one says 'I know Kung Fu,' and one is replied to with the words, 'Show me,' one is quoting, and being quoted from, the cult movie by the Wachowski brothers, The Matrix. This seminal movie from the late nineties had no aliens in it. "Bullet time" was introduced to the 'big screen' by this film, which was slick and stylish. The trilogy can be purchased using ASIN B000BHZ1DS, although the sequels (The Matrix Reloaded and The Matrix Revolutions) fail to live up to the groundbreaking mindblowing spectacle of the first movie.

[7] Parkour, or "free running" is the invention of the superfit David Belle, a Frenchman who leaps from tall buildings and runs up walls, all for real. For examples of his work, please see District 13 (or Banlieue 13, the original French title) starring David Belle in person and co-starring Cyril Raffaelli, or District 13: Ultimatum (Banlieue 13: Ultimatum) starring David Belle and Cyril Raffaelli again. The Frenchmen in the movie speak in French in the movie, which sounds a little gay, but there is also a dubbed version. If you only watch one film this year, watch District 13 too. The set of movies comes in a box, a "boxset" if you will, under the ASIN B002KAIVU4. Disclaimer: there are no aliens in this movie. For a movie bearing the title "District" followed by "a number" and featuring aliens, the reader is directed towards District 9 written and directed by Neill Blomkamp (amongst others) with the ASIN B002KCNT3G. This movie features aliens and also South African accents.

his everso benevolent eyes. He had to show more, give more, be more benevolent. He needed a big gesture. So he invited the twins to his house for the following Sunday's family dinner. No staff member had ever been invited to Sunday family dinner. Aware that no staff member had ever been invited to Sunday family dinner and to avoid being considered as having any paedophilic overtones in the invitation he also invited their cousin Proctor. Proctor was a faithful worker; he always ironed his shirt and kept his hair short enough to not be able to tell if it was dirty. The tattoos didn't half scare the punters too. All in all, Proctor was an all right bouncer. He had hard eyes too, although they had an unclean look to them of late, but that was none of the benevolent Drug Overlord Boss's business. It didn't interfere with his keeping the punters under control and, to top it all, he was never shy about battering any punter that needed it and it probably wouldn't do any harm to promote him to Senior Bouncer.

The benevolent Overlord Boss Local Godfather had a name but it was a secret. He went by Luigi even though he was 43rd generation British and had as much Italian blood in him as the people that ran the Kebab Shoppe. Luigi had a wife whose name was also a secret but who went by Maria. Luigi had a daughter who was a secret but whose name wasn't. Her name was Sofia Mancini (pronounced So-fee-ahh Man-chee-nay) and she dined with her parents every Sunday even though the world in general was unaware that Luigi and Maria had a grown up daughter and she always kept her parentage under wraps. It wouldn't have taken the genius of Poirot to work out the relationship, but no one cared enough to bother: no one asked her any questions so she told no lies. Sofia Mancini was deeply talented and highly successful and had never once traded on her father's reputation.

Maria, who had less Italian blood in her than her husband, that is to say, about as much as native Inuits who thought the year was only one day long and didn't invent alloyed metal, cooked hearty minestrone soup from the old country with celery, kidney beans, pasta shells, tomatoes – lots of tomatoes! – pureed tomatoes, turnip, scallops, parmesan, potatoes, leeks, onions and okra, topped with enough black pepper to choke a small child. The soup was stewed and reduced until it had to be eaten with a knife and fork like hard food. She cooked lasagne and garlic bread, both in an unordinary but still a good and tasty way, and pretended to prepare tiramisu, which she actually bought from Tesco's Finest range. All women have their limitation, hers was desserts. She accepted her limitation, as not accepting her limitations was not one of her limitations, and so she resorted to buying dessert. Everyone was happier with something they could eat that didn't strip their insides out as it passed through their digestive tract. There had been the occasional salmonella scare before she knew that desserts were her limitation. When God was giving out dessert making abilities "Maria" (God knows her real name but isn't going to tell you) was in the line for the restrooms.

The Sunday of the family dinner with invited minions was upon them; the dessert was bought and decanted from the Tesco box, the soup was a day old and the lasagne bubbled in the oven, yielding its rawness forever. The Wrong Order Twins got up at 5am and went for a run with weighted ankles and wrists. They removed the shackles and ran over the rooftops faster than the sun could rise. Proctor also rose at 5am, as he had to make a stop at the West Country before the privileged invited family dinner. He and Veronica headed off at 5.15am, Veronica with a fresh supply of enzyme action washing powder, paid by cash, from Tesco, Morrisons and Waitrose this time in case anyone in Asda was getting suspicious, along with more sausage rolls and some limeade for the journey.

The man previously referred to in the present tense and who now could only accurately be described as a man in the past tense, but still, for the sake of convenience called Mr D. Ville, was decomposing at a nicely augmented rate. The superaction soap suds were digesting his skin and organs. Veronica had no reason to fear the dead body. No one really has any reason to fear a dead body, but most will be squeamish about them, especially, as in the case of the recently deceased Mr D. Ville, a dead body with half a face eaten away by microscopic organisms, with the eyeballs only barely attached and resting on the cheekbones, staring in a demented, tortured way at her wherever she moved. She ran away the old cold water, strips of flesh flaking off the corpse into the whirlpool of the plug. She scooped out the bigger chunks to let the water run away almost completely and then sprinkled the remains of the botched body with all three large boxes of washing powder, rerunning a nice, warm bath. The body snapped, crackled and popped as the bubbles once again consumed it. Operation Decompose The Dead Man was going well. She had hired the cottage for six weeks; at his present rate of accelerated decomposition that should be workable. Proctor honked his horn to hurry his sister. Veronica made sure the majority of what was left of Mr Ville was submerged and encouraged him to keep up the good job of disappearing out of existence and into the Devonshire waste water system, 'There's a good man.'

Chapter, the TwentySecond
Family Values

Neither Proctor nor Veronica Dempsey lost any sleep – metaphorically speaking – over their West Country excursions. They both lost sleep – literally speaking – because they had to travel through the night the first time they went and very early in the morning on the second visit, totalling approximately 8 hours of lost sleep. But metaphorically speaking they didn't lose sleep, that is to say, they slept the sleep of those blessed with a clear conscience, or, to be more specific in the Dempsey offspring case, those even more blessed with no conscience to speak of. The decomposing body of the man previously alive and would still potentially be alive were it not for VD's narcotic filled loft did not encroach on either of the Dempsey's waking thoughts or dreaming wanderings, save to make logistical plans for buying more washing powder and what time to leave on a Sunday morning. Proctor Dempsey drove Veronica home in a non-judgemental way and went to his rented flat to shower before dinner. Shower temperature: tepid. Towel: once white when it lived in a hotel, now grey because it lived with Proctor. The tepid water bounced off his inked shoulders and chest. His legs were too white. He should get more work done, but what would Michael Schofield do? When Proctor wasn't aiding and abetting his sister in her criminal activities he thought non-stop about his goddess of enigma. He called her Butterfly instead of 'the woman who lives on Gardener Street with the tattoo that looks a bit like a butterfly' because he didn't know her name and he must call her something. He thought about her while he showered and he imagined past the part where she opened the door in see-through black lingerie. He imagined she smiled on him and nodded for him to come in: he couldn't imagine her voice; he wouldn't know how to start. He imagined her walk and what she smelled like through her see-through attire, but no matter how often and how hard he tried he could not imagine any further. He tried to superimpose memories he had of other women but his brain refused to merge the sensation of Butterfly with any other caterpillar creature. He could not imagine touching or kissing her. His brain said no and looped back to the start whenever his lips got too close to hers or he reached out to untie her see-through gown. The tepid shower washed him and the grey towel dried him.

What do people wear to family Sunday dinner with the boss and his wife and secret daughter that he knew nothing about? He had his court suit, that is to say, the suit he wore when he went to court. It still fitted him. Was it too fancy? What would Michael Schofield do? He was a genius, he would know. If Proctor wore his black trousers and a white shirt he'd look like he was going bouncing. Would that be construed as disrespectful? Perhaps. Or it may show that he's dedicated. He put the court suit on. Stifling, m'lud. He put his work clothes on. His body bulked up. Like a salivating Pavlov's dog, he wanted to hit someone. He put on black jogging trousers and a black AC/DC t-shirt with long sleeves. Comfortable. Smart. Sorted. He drove in his comfy clothes to the twins' house. The comfy clothes made the journey faster, but not literally. The twins both wore black trousers and black jumpers because it made them feel ninja, literally.

They made small talk in the car, 'What's your mother up to these days?' Proctor asked.

'Dunno,' they replied aloud together, 'Yours?'

'Still in prison,' he answered.

'Oh yeah,' they said together, 'that's funny.'

The mother of the Wrong Order Ninja Twins was thoroughly enjoying her new career as a prostitute. She couldn't understand why anyone would bother with a normal job, with time constraints and boss people and annoying co-workers and measly pay and early mornings and cold crowded buses when they could do what she did. They could have sex for money. She would giggle to herself when men gave her £40 and then gave her cock too. It was like the best two for one deal ever (which, incidentally, she also did for money). Money then sex. Why didn't everyone do it all the time? Money, excellent, then sex, excellenter. That's what Natalie – no longer in need of a particular man, many men were better – Smyth had been up to these days. There was the downside of regular trips to the gum clinic for check-ups, but Natalie made friends with the nurses so that she could categorise it as a social outing. The twins had no idea their mother had become a whore. The mother had no idea the twins were training to kill with their bare hands. The force was strong with that pair.

'How's cousin Veronica?' The twins asked together.

Proctor considered for a moment what would happen if he told them their marginally mental cousin who waddled like a drunkard on the line of genius and madness had fallen onto the side of madness, inventing some drug-like substance and then possibly killing a random guy, no, private investigator, and regardless of the dubious nature of the killing she was definitely heavily involved in the cover up, but instead he said, 'Fine.'

Proctor Dempsey, black jogging trousers and black heavy metal t-shirt, and the Wrong Order Twins, black trousers and black jumpers, all exited the once red, now orange, car. The gravel registered the presence of Proctor alone, scrunching to the rhythm of one set of footsteps. The twins were becoming more Ninja than Wrong Order. Proctor rang the bell, pausing for a nanosecond with his finger at the buzzer remembering the last bell he almost rang.

The twins looked at each other and smiled a secret smile, telepathically saying, 'This'll be fun!' and answering, 'I know, right?' Footsteps approached. Proctor's body became alert as the strings in his cells vibrated at the same resonance as the person who was now opening the door. It was her: perfection, enigma, Butterfly.

Chapter, the TwentyThird
Salt & Pepper

When faced with your fantasy, your options are limited. Fainting is an option, if you're a woman from the 1920s. Proctor wasn't, wasn't and therefore didn't. Accepting that you are facing your fantasy here in the real world is an option, if you're a methodical thinker and can quickly rationalise a situation. Proctor wasn't, couldn't and therefore didn't. Proctor plumped for the only other option available, the remaining option for the hard of thinking; he thought he was in a fantasy, even though 15 seconds before he was fairly certain he was driving his car with his multi-gendered twin cousins. As a fantasy, it wasn't his best since she was wearing actual clothes. Awesome clothes. Black jeans and a black and pink corset. And she was still amazing. Why had he fantasised her in clothes, awesomeness notwithstanding? As he pondered his strange new fantasy she spoke.

'Well, this is a surprise,' she said. 'AC/DC: retro.' Did he just fantasise her voice? This fantasy was getting out of hand. Did he bang his head getting out the car? Did he crash the car en-route? He did a good job of her voice it had to be said; it was exactly as he imagined it would sound, if he was brave enough to allow himself to imagine how it would sound. It sounded like rich, dark chocolate and a spicy tannin laden Pinot Noir.

'Hello,' the Wrong Order/Ninja borderline Ninja/Wrong Order Twins said in unison.

'Well, aren't you two adorable?' she said with a whisper of sarcasm through her chocolate covered voice.

Shit, the twins were in the fantasy too? Why would he do that? He just wouldn't do that. Would he? No. Ergo, this wasn't a fantasy. Ergo, she was standing right in front of him. Ergo, he should faint. But he still wasn't, wasn't, so didn't. His unclean eyes were washed clean with her light reflection. He really ought to say something, since he had got around to accepting that he was facing his fantasy in his real life.

'This is a surprise,' he said at last.

'I'm so glad we have an accord,' she smiled at him, giving him a whiff of her spicy soul, 'Well, I suppose you all better come in, all those favoured by the baron Luigi.'

Maria greeted them in the enthusiastic way she supposed Sicilian mamas greeted guests, with a bear hug and a kiss on each cheek. The twins found her to be squishy. Proctor had never had a friendly hug off a woman before and he instantly became a fan of the fake Italian squishy woman. Luigi insisted on being called Luigi, although no one ever called him anything else, and introduced Maria and Sofia to his guests: 'You must call me Luigi, I insist,' he said in his best barest fake Italian accent, 'this is my wife Maria and my daughter Sofia.'

'Sofia,' Proctor said looking at Butterfly. 'So-fee-ya. Soaf-eeya. Soafeeahh. So-fi-ya. Sofa-ya.'

'Dad, make him stop,' Sofia said.

'Proctor, that's a bit mental, stop doing that,' her dad obliged.

'Proctor?' Sofia laughed. 'Proc-tor. Pro-ac-tor. Proc-tir. Proctor?'

'Luigi,' Proctor said in complaint.

'Sofia,' Luigi obliged him.

'Sofia,' Proctor said.

'Proctor,' Sofia said.

'Luke,' Leia said.
'Leia?' Luke said.
'Luigi,' Maria said.
'Sofia,' Proctor said again.
'Proctor,' Sofia said again.
'Do you two know each other?' Luigi asked.
'Do we sound like we know each other?' Sofia answered.
'A little bit,' Maria said.
'No,' Proctor answered.

'My daughter does all manner of weird shit for money,' Luigi said, 'pardon my Italian there with the shit word. There's no telling who she knows. But she's been an independent woman since the age of 18, never asked for a penny, so I couldn't be prouder.'

'Thanks dad,' Sofia said.

'What sort of weird shit?' Luke asked.

'All sorts,' Maria answered for her, 'but we don't talk about it at the dinner table. Let's eat.'

Proctor Dempsey was unable to take trains. He didn't get motion sickness in them, he didn't have a traumatic experience as a child with Thomas The Tank Engine or Percy, the green evil one, but when he stood at a train platform he always wanted to jump in front of the train to see what it would be like. It wasn't a conscious want, he never thought, 'I wonder what death by train would feel like?', but he had to fight his suicidal brain every time to not step onto the tracks. Where most people's default brain setting would be "don't step into the road of an oncoming train", his default setting was "walk in front of the train, ah, go on", it was a struggle to not. He wasn't known for his great intellect, but one of the smartest things he ever did was to stop taking trains. Arguably it was no smarter than any animal's self preservation instinct, like an octopus spraying ink or wolves hunting in packs or the Predator using extreme camouflage technology making it invisible. Proctor also never took buses. He did get motion sickness in them and once, when he was a child, a drunk urinated in the seat beside him and the warm wetness reached his school trousers, the smell and the motion making him throw up all down his school shirt and tie. His mum was pregnant with Veronica at the time and shouted at him for getting his tie dirty; it had to be hand washed.

'What're you thinking about?' Sofia asked Proctor, hearing his spirit sink and gurgle.

'Just something that happened when I was a kid,' he replied.

Sofia listened as his spirit drowned in his words. She reached out, put her hand on top of his, giving him breath again and said, 'This isn't the time.'

After the store-bought dessert, round of applause for Tesco's finest, the Ninja Twins entertained the grown-ups with some of their Kung Fu. They moved like water. There was no beginning or end to them. They chopped and kicked, blocked and dodged, swept and bowed, sweated and breathed.

'Oh bravo!' Maria clapped energetically, 'What clever children! Like the multiple birth children we never had!'

Luigi, Sofia and Proctor joined in the applause.

'Your turn, Proctor,' Sofia said, 'how are you going to entertain us?'

'I can do one-handed press-ups,' he said.

'Show us that!' Maria said, excitedly. She was overtired from the fun afternoon.

'No, don't,' Sofia said, 'how about you show us your tattoos instead?'

'I don't think that would be appropriate,' Luigi said, not wanting to offend himself by looking at a man's torso, 'anyway, there's been enough entertainment.'

Maria offered coffee to her guests, which Sofia dutifully made with a little help from Proctor. Proctor didn't suffer from nerves (whether he was good in the boxing ring because of it or as a result of it is undetermined due to lack of control data). He therefore didn't understand the feeling in his stomach because he had no reference point for his brain to associate it with. It wasn't heartburn. It wasn't cramp. It wasn't wind. It wasn't stomach flu. It wasn't appendicitis. It wasn't diarrhoea. He felt something though, a queasy stomach tightening sensation that wasn't heartburn, cramp, wind, stomach flu, appendicitis or diarrhoea. It was because he was going to be alone with Butterfly. Or maybe it was the lasagne. Or maybe it was the West Country air he consumed that morning. But maybe it was love, or something very closely related to it.

She asked him to take his shirt off without making it a question, 'Take your t-shirt off.'

'How long?' She asked, scanning his artwork from a distance at first. His stomach tightened as she came in for a closer look. His calves started to sweat.

'12 hours.'

'How many sessions?'

'One.'

With an approving smile that could launch a hundred thousand dreams she said, 'One? Très cool.'

She stood right in front of him, tracing the lines and hidden passages in the design. The top of his feet started sweating as well. His stomach stopped being a stomach and became an organ made of antimatter. There was a lot of work on his body and although it wasn't high art it wasn't awful. One session was impressive; he must be a machine. She ran her tongue across the width of his back; he tasted human, he tasted like rare cooked steak and Hob Nobs. She lay on the kitchen floor.

She asked him to show her his one-handed press-ups, without asking a question, 'Show me your one-handed press-ups.' He did it. Although, as previously mentioned, he was not known for his great thinking, he assumed since she lay on the floor she meant for him to do the press-ups on top of her. It would be an embarrassing mistake if he was wrong, one that he would probably never recover from in her universe-perfect eyes. He wasn't wrong in his assumption. She wanted him right above him and watched his inked torso as he brought it down close to her, almost touching, then drew it away again.

'Sofia! What's going on here?' Her dad yelled – the coffee would have made itself faster – 'Leave my staff alone! This was not a solicitation session!'

Sofia pulled Proctor down on top of her and kissed him. His rare cooked steak complimented her Pinot Grigio and their superstring section crescendoed together.

'Sorry,' Luigi said and backed out carefully, 'my mistake. Sorry. Carry on.'

Chapter, the TwentyFourth
Conversations With Beelzebub

To return, for the time being, to the matter at hand, the matter of the prepared poppy powder, tested as yet only once by its creator, the shyly uninterested Veronica Could Be A Genius, Time Will Reveal All Dempsey. The unorthodox beauty Sofia 'The Butterfly' Mancini and her relationship with each of the Dempsey males will be a topic again soon, suffice it to say for the present that Luigi knew that Sofia was not soliciting Proctor because of, and in the event of, the kiss – SM did not kiss clients. Ever.

A bigger scale production of Veronica's Secret Side Chain Opium was underway under the university's roof. Her coworkers didn't notice that she had opened a new chain of research since they were as equally uninterested in what she did as she was in them. They pottered about as usual with their mediocre chemicals performing mediocre transformations under mediocre conditions with mediocre efficiency. Meanwhile Veronica Dempscy replicated her superior reaction conditions with her superior chemicals. Doc Barta Savage – the one and only! – monitored Veronica in a superior fashion. She had opened up a discussion line with her appropriate colleagues who knew more about the road to pharmaceuticals than she did. They told her how long and hard it was. They told her the shockingly poor success rate of potential drug molecules. They told her that her little research lab wasn't up to the epic journey. They told her she would fail in her quest. They told her she was stupid. They told her it wouldn't look good in her annual review. They told her she may as well give up the chemistry lark and open a sex line. She kept note of everything they said, who, when, what intonation, knowing that when she got her Nobel Prize and the inevitable invite to the Royal Society she would subsequently black ball every one of them. Bastard colleagues. They'd pay for their lack of faith. She was Doctor Barta Savage, didn't they know. Doctor Barta Savage The Educated. Doctor Barta Savage, The Doctor of Bronze, Brains and Tits. She was ballsy and shouty and always got her way. Any time she didn't get her way it obviously wasn't important anyway. She always got her way on important things and things she could remember.

The private investigator never bothered asking for the bonus he earned off her, as per their agreement, the full legalities of which are unimportant and lengthy and the law is so desperately dull it need not be mentioned in any more detail other than to remark that although Doc Savage had paid Mr D. Ville (as he was then known and is still currently unknown to not be known by it any longer by the general populous, including the ballsy Doctor) for services rendered, there was the opportunity for a bonus in the event of good work. His work was sound, thus Doc Savage assumed he must have been a humanitarian with altruistic motives, his reward being to have helped her. To the best of Veronica Dempsey's knowledge no one came looking or went looking for the pointy-toothed detective. That was a stroke of luck. Doc Savage got to keep more of her money in her pile of enough money anyway. Arguably the more important outcome, for the Dempseys at any rate, was that no one came looking or went looking for the man that had died in the Dempsey's loft of an overdose of illegally prepared illegal substance, thereby foregoing the unfortunate circumstance of Veronica having to lie to some fuzz. As VD increased her efficiency in the manufacture of her magenta opium and BS made a mental note of all the careers she had to destroy, the private dick was obligingly returning to his ground state of decomposed molecules several hundred miles away, past the Seven Seas of Rhye.

The Devil looks like Danny Kaye. That's a little known fact. The Devil that appeared to Veronica Dempsey in a vision – was it a vision? – looked like Danny Kaye, star of such feel good post Second World War movies as The Court Jester, Hans Christian Anderson and the likes. The lovable, affable, fair-haired, soft-featured actor. He didn't introduce himself as the Devil, nor as a man of wealth and taste. Nor as Danny Kaye. Nor as evil with a capital D. No introductions were made, the Danny Kaye Devil just materialised for a chat and then left. He flattered Veronica by telling her he had heard great things about her in the future. Flattery didn't register with Veronica Dempsey. At first Veronica wondered if hallucinations were a side effect of the drug, but she took it too long ago for it still to be having a physiological application. She then wondered if hallucinations were a side effect of watching someone die and then removing and destroying the body, but that seemed like the sort of thing that happened to people with an active conscience.

'You're not hallucinating,' Beelzebub assured her.

'I bet all hallucinations say that,' she replied.

As no introductions were made Veronica was unaware that she was talking to the actual Devil. The Devil probably doesn't carry a passport; he has no desire to try and get into heaven. She also had no idea who Danny Kaye was, so she didn't think she was talking to him either. The Satanic stranger invited her out for a drink.

'How about a drink?' he said.

'I'm not thirsty,' she replied.

'I wish I'd met you earlier,' he said back.

'I've been here all day,' she replied.

He posed the sneaky trick question the FBI use to ascertain a killer's instinct, just for fun:

'I know a woman. She went to her mum's funeral,' he began,

'there's a man there, at the funeral, that she has never seen before and he infatuates her. She falls instantly in love. The following day the woman kills her very own sister-'

'Ah, clever.' Veronica mused.

'Clever, indeed? Why do you say that?' Danny Devil asked.

'To see him again. But I apologise for interrupting,' she said, 'Continue.'

'I'm done,' he replied with a wickedly handsome smile. She was ripe and her brainwaves were delectable. Her sinusoidal brain activity was steady, almost flat. Most "normal" people (those the FBI would not be interested in their answer to the trick question), to elaborate, those born without the killer instinct, are prone to manufacture all manner of ludicrous connections between "the sister" and "the man" and provide answers like "they were married" to attempt to justify the murder. Veronica saw no furious need for the sister to have anything to do with the man. The Danny Kaye Doppelganger of Evil was satisfied with her simplistic reasoning that if the man was at a family funeral then the man might attend another family funeral – motive enough for murder. If you're a psychopath.

'It's a pity I no longer take wives,' he said as he started to fade out of her plane of existence, 'but I suppose you're better here.'

Veronica was not perturbed by her encounter with the Prince of Darkness, he seemed pleasant enough and gave no vibes of being the incarnation of Evil. She filed the experience away in her head as a real seeming hallucination, and one she wouldn't mind having repeated on account of the fact his conversation didn't bore her and stories normally bore her. Why fear the Devil when he looks like Danny Kaye and just wants a chat? No overtures of doom accompanied the hallucination's entrance and exit, no supernatural manifestations, no rending of limbs, no red hot pokers in the arse, no wailing, no inexplicable chills, weeping or gnashing of teeth. Veronica Dempsey, as soon as the encounter was appropriately stored in her supercomputerbrain, promptly ceased thinking about the whole thing and slowly measured 50 millilitres of hallucinogenic-inducing-toluene.

Satan was pleased with his visit to the Dempsey girl. Satan is a very busy creature and not everyone on Earth can claim to have had the honour of his company. While he was in the area he decided to call on Doctor Barta Savage to ensure she was up to the task ahead of her.

'Aren't you Danny Kaye?' Doc Savage shouted when he entered her office without knocking. 'Oh, wait, he must be about a hundred by now and you can't be over 50.'

'33.'

'No, really? But I'm 33 and you look twenty years older than me.'

'Right. Excellent.' Satan was, again, satisfied. She seemed up to her role amicably. Just to be sure he sang a little ditty as he left:

'Barta Savage, cleverest of all; Barta Savage, heed the call; You're the star of your story; Don't let anyone steal your glory!'

The Devil, who looks like Danny Kaye, left the campus. He could have called on the cleaners to see if they were at it again, but that would have been like checking on the course of the midday sun. Of course they were at it again. They were always at it. Who watches the cleaners? Other cleaners. And who watches them? Other cleaners. And them? Others. Let he who has never known adversity sit down and shut up. He is not fit to judge them. Saskia Suffolk was in charge of the less than moral operations. She invented the less than moral operations. Despite having a husband who claimed to love her for who she was, exactly as she was, she knew she was less than she should be. Through no fault of her own, Saskia Suffolk had to have her ass cheeks surgically removed. She was left with a concave butt. A woman with a concave butt is like a circus without a bearded lady. An abomination. She felt it strongly and she felt deeply. Her breast was ample, not massive, but not the smallest boobs on the block, but that was no consolation for the non-existent ass.

The first time "it" happened "it" was an accident and the morality surrounding an accident is abstract at best. The second time was not an accident and the morality was less than impeccable. But it felt good and for a time she forgot about her hollow bum.

The cleaners partook in what is known in the industry as "oxygen licking". They were, by extension, known as "oxygen lickers". Oxygen licking, as everyone knows, is the practise of opening up oxygen canisters and lapping the euphoric gas (oxygen is a gas at standard temperatures and pressures). The oxygen, unlike its so-called Noble Gas friend helium, leaves the voice box in tact. It by-passes the throat in general and goes straight for the party in the lungs. When no-one's looking oxygen is the wildest element of all, living it up in the lungs then rollercoasting around the body on the river Heme. It takes the party with it, filling all the dull places with wild fun – the brain wakes up, the ovaries (or testes, the role of cleaners is not a gender specific workforce any longer, albeit the men always forget to refill the papertowels in the laboratories and are generally not as good at it) fire, the senses sharpen, the ass feels less hollow, the life feels less hopeless.

As well as the pleasant psychological aspect, oxygen has other, less adorable, qualities, like its explosive power. The question of morality arises from the stealing aspect. Oxygen doesn't grow on trees[8]. It costs money. The cleaners don't pay for it, ergo, it is stealing, ergo, of moral disrepute. Cleaners can't go around helping themselves to whatever chemicals they feel like, whenever they feel like it, or all academics would become cleaners.

---

[8] According to the laws of pedantry, it should be pointed out that oxygen, aka O_2, or, to give it its scientific name, dimolecular oxygen, does, of course, come from green plant photosynthesis, which trees can, naturally, contribute to. No alchemy is involved: oxygen does come from trees, but it is not "grown" therein.

Chapter, the TwentyFifth
Love Life

Before time was invented people were happier. They weren't late for appointments, they didn't miss trains, there was no such thing as a 9–5 existence, eggs took as long as suited you for them to cook, there were no twee calendars of ugly kittens, all for example. There were some less happy aspects, like traffic lights and their sporadic nature, and missing the start of movies, but on the whole people were happier. People that weren't the Swiss, that is, were happier with their leisurely doing whatever, whenever, it didn't matter; things got done when things got done without "when" being a concept. All was well with the world. Until the Swiss decided something was missing. Someone moved their cheese and they took a wicked revenge by inventing time. No one knew the liberties they were giving up and embraced "time" like penicillin after the a severe batch of the clap. It seemed like an affable enough affair, until the library shut at eight o'clock when you weren't finished looking through the shelves, but it shut anyway for no reason other than it being eight o'clock. People started dying of old age. Buses, for the large part, ignored the new fangled time idea, but trains fell in love with it to varying degrees based on location. The Japanese trains, for example, had a passionate love tryst with time and they became virtually inseparable, like

Siamese twins. The Italian trains didn't hate it, but could take it or leave it, depending on mood. The British attempted to incorporate time into their train schedule because they liked being told what to do and apologise when they weren't able to live up to their rules in a positively British way. Proctor Dempsey never travelled on buses because of a traumatic childhood experience involving a drunk man, warm urine, his school trousers and subsequent gastric expulsion of his school lunch down his tie, and avoided trains because of the overwhelming desire to feel Death by Locomotive that standing on a train platform brought out in him. Following his kiss with Sofia Mancini – the kiss that lasted a lifetime in the space of less than thirty seconds – Proctor's death wish had vanished. To test the hypothesis he stood at the train platform that very night, daring the trains to whoosh up to the station while he stood his ground. As Proctor hadn't ventured near a train station since his childhood he can be forgiven for being unaware that Sundays on the British Railways were like a partial holiday. As such, and after standing for over an hour without a hint of any trains coming or going, Proctor got bored and went home. Had a train come along there's an eighty percent chance he wouldn't have had any urge to jump. He had a purpose. He didn't know how long it would last, but he currently had a purpose to live – to get to know her more. To get to know Butterfly, real name Sofia Mancini. He asked her if he could call her Butterfly. She said it wasn't very original. He countered by saying neither was calling her by her real name. She succumbed to his persuasive argument with a smile that could launch a hundred thousand recoveries.

Following Sunday family dinner, the entertainment by the Ninja Twins' Kung Fu routine, and the impromptu kiss that lasted a lifetime but ended after about thirty seconds, Sofia told Proctor she would like to get to know him better. She liked the cut of his jib, if not the artistry of his tats.

'I don't really know how to have a normal relationship,' Proctor confided.

'Then let's not have one,' she said. 'Sex?'

'Now?' he asked

'Yesterday?' she said.

'Yesterday?' he repeated.

'Now,' she said.

There was a pause when there should have been undressing.

'Because of your dad?' she asked.

'I can't help thinking about him and you. You and him. You and he. He and you.' Proctor also confided.

'Oh, sweet boy, I assure you, I won't be thinking about him. And I assure you, neither will you.' He was assured.

She was right. Sofia Mancini, his Butterfly, the pale goddess with the powers of Aphrodite herself showed him what his function in life was. His mind never wandered to Gardener Street, not even once. She held him in her eyes and kept him in the present and in the room for every second. She floated around him, she took hold of his body and shook all traces of inadequacies out it, she dripped real sweat on his satiated, ink-scarred skin. She was right. He had no other reason to have been born than to spend that time in her. She was right.

'That's enough for tonight,' she said when they were finished anyway. 'I'm going home.'

'But it's your night off,' he said.

'Okay, stalker,' she said recovering her nakedness, 'but I have other things to do.'

'Won't you stay?' he asked.

'You want me to stay over on our first date? Not even a date, on our first pre-date? What do you think I am, some two-bit whore?'

'What are you?'

'I'm free,' she said.

'You're amazing,' he said.

'I'm free,' she repeated.

She left, like she said. He remained in the sweat-damp bed. His mind replayed and then played again her magnificence. Then he played it again. And then again. She was his proof that God existed. Only a Supreme Being could construct something so perfect and make her more than the sum of her parts. Mortals were made of protons, electrons and neutrons, and maybe they were made of strings or quarks or bales of hay, but hers were made of freedom and joy. He got dressed, energised by Her, and went to the train track to prove how little he would be drawn to suicide. The lack of trains on a Sunday didn't quash his spirit. As he was not scientifically gifted he still considered the experiment a success, even without the catalyst of death (that is, the train).

Chapter, the TwentySixth
Collision Course

In the happenstance that is life, there are several things that can lead to a satisfactory existence. Low intellect is one – if you're too stupid to know that life sucks then it won't. Finding true love is said to be one, but who in life ever achieves that? The odds against it are so astronomically high to be statistically insignificant, ergo, impossible. Not improbable, impossible. And that's before you even take into account whether love exists. Those of a modest to high intellect are therefore left with the option of finding out early on in life what they are good at and engineering a way to make a living at it. Those born with the extraordinary ability to be miserable better than anyone else on the planet have been dealt a bum lot and should be pitied, but as they've invariably got that covered themselves the next best plan is to avoid them where possible. The best of the best of the miserable will probably become writers and revel in it anyway.

Peter O'Shaughnessy, hitherto not mentioned by full name, but not unfamiliar to the reader, was fairly good at a number of things. He was good at cycling, which naturally meant he was good at annoying drivers and almost getting killed daily. He was good at chatting up lonely and/or desperate women on the internet and having a go of them without their husband's knowledge, mainly by telling them about his firm buttocks and offering them a touch, under the internet moniker Firm_Buttock_Pete. Lonely and/or desperate women on the internet were a soft touch for the hard touch. These were things he chose not to make a living at and enjoyed in a recreational sense. His chosen profession involved subterfuge, which he often employed recreationally in his quest to bed married women, without letting on to his wife in the process. His brain was not as sharply cut as his ass and he was not good at remembering the names of the women he had exercised his butt on, but, in his defence, they did now number in the high hundreds. With hundreds of lonely and/or desperate women having been had a go of by Firm_Buttock_Pete then, in fairness, it should be iterated that even if he had been good with names there's a good chance the name Dempsey would have been long forgotten. His sexing of the senior Dempsey female was in excess of eight years previously, back in the stone ages of dial-up. He would have trouble remembering an ex-wife's name after that long. So when he was given his new assignment in Subterfuge there wasn't even a semblance of a thought that there might be a conflict. He had shagged a hamlet worth of people, in his defence. He read the assignment. Interesting enough. Subterfuge, high probability of sandwiches and overnight stayaways meant an even higher probability of Firm_Buttock_Pete getting some new action. In his defence, the quality of woman he was able to subterfuge into a touch of his firm ass was deteriorating along with their pelvic control. He had to keep quantities high to make up for lack of quality among the aged. The assignment itself was certainly not too hard sounding. He took the assignment since he had one of two choices: take the assignment or quit. Peter O'Shaughnessy (aka very same Firm_Buttock_Pete of the internet fame, he who seduced and left Jessica Dempsey/Rabbit after a very brief encounter in a Travelodge when she was still in fairly good internal condition) had a poor working relationship with his boss, and his boss didn't even know that Pete had had a go of his wife. His boss was always looking for an excuse to fire his (mighty firm) ass, but Pete was, unfortunately, fairly good at his job and he was a Union Boy.

*

Pauline Burns, who cosmetically whitened her teeth to the brink of an ultraviolet catastrophe, was the first to arrive at lab 7-14.

'Oh. My. God,' she said when she saw the mess. 'Oh. My. God. Oh. My. God. Oh. My. God.'

At first glance it looked like there had been an explosion. The lab had been lovingly redecorated in essence of glass. Pauline Burns was still standing – 'Oh. My. God. Oh. My. God.' – when Davey Jones arrived.

'What the hell happened?' he asked.

'I don't know!' she yelped, 'It wasn't me!'

'Alright, calm it, I wasn't accusing you!'

Pauline Burns and Davey Jones were still standing – 'Oh. My. God. Oh. My. God.' 'Savage'll go mental when she sees it!' – when Veronica Dempsey arrived.

'What a mess,' she said. 'There's broken glass everywhere.'

'Yep,' Davey Jones replied.

Pauline Burns, Davey Jones and Veronica Dempsey were all still standing – 'Oh. My. God. Oh. My. God.' 'When the boss gets here we're all dead!' 'Broken glass, hm.' – when Doctor Barta Savage, master of all she surveyed, including mess, happened by.

'Oh dear Christ!' she yelled, 'What's been going on here?'

'It wasn't us,' Pauline Burns's ludicrously white teeth protested.

'Yes, thank you, Captain Flipping Obvious,' Doc Savage shouted louder than her normal shouting volume by four factors, 'have any of you reported this yet?'

No one had. Doc Savage's voice, which was categorised as "too loud" in the ground state, could be heard by the Security men two buildings away without the need of a telephone. They complained of temporary threshold shift and sued. Next she phoned the head of department. Then she phoned the Dean of the Faculty. Finally she phoned the Principal of the University, since she didn't have the Prime Minister's number to hand. She made noise from the bottom to the top and she shouted from the soul of her stomach and the stomach of her soul.

'What sort of institution is this? The place has been ransacked! What do we pay Security for? Fun? Monkeys would do a better job securing the place! Monkeys would do a better job running the place! Yes, you heard me. And I'll tell you something else as well, this would never have happened if a woman was in charge. Yes, you heard me. This place is a disaster. This would never have happened in my day. Yes, you heard! I need a cleaning crew. I need compensation from the monkeys that swan about with Security badges on. I need guarantees that someone will be brought to account over this! I need – what did you say? How dare you! It was not one of mine!'

The security tapes were reviewed since that's what they're there for, but as they only covered entrances and the odd corridor here and there they were next to useless. They were more a deterrent than a useful security measure or investigative tool. No one had entered the university in a suspicious hoody with the slogan RANSACKER on it, so that line of investigation had to be dropped. There were too many normal looking people in the world. If someone really wanted to, someone could have entered the university during peak time undetected, hide out in an unmonitored location (which was most of them) until everyone left and then be free to do the nasty on Doc Savage's lab, simply leaving the following day during rush time, completely undetected in their subterfuge ways. Someone would really have to want to do that as it required an overnight stay, which meant a modicum of planning would likely be involved. With sandwiches. Fortunately Peter O'Shaughnessy didn't mind overnight stays, loved egg mayonnaise sandwiches and he got off on planning.

His plan hadn't altogether gone "to plan" as "the plan" hadn't involved ransacking the place. "The plan" was for a quick in and out, no questions asked, thank you ma'am, oh baby, retrieve and extract, but he couldn't find anything he was sent to retrieve, so extracting became difficult. His searching became furious as "the plan" slipped away and he became frantic in his kidneys. Furious, frantic kidneys led to accidents with the assorted laboratory glassware. Once he'd smashed a few things by accident he took to smashing things on purpose, making the whole event look more like an act of vandalism than something with a retrieve and extract purpose. Vandalise The Place thus became incorporated into "the plan". It was fun, too. He read through mundane laboratory notebooks one last time and took pointless samples off the benches. Perhaps his employers had been misinformed? Not his problem. If what he wanted wasn't there, there was nought he could do about it. He couldn't extract and retrieve nothingness. The lab books all told the same story – mediocre chemistry, nothing useable by his employers or the chemistry community at large. Even the prime target Veronica Dempsey's lab book was filled with averageness. What a waste of his time. Did they want him to retrieve the neatest, most anal lab book in the history of chemistry? He could manage that, but nothing at all of interest.

The police arrived shortly after ten. Doc Savage took Veronica Dempsey aside and told her not to tell them what she had been working on secretly. Veronica understood the concept of secrets; she had no more intention of telling them about her Super Secret Opium than she had of telling them about the Super Secret Dead Body Accelerated Decomposition Operation.

Chapter, the TwentySeventh
Very Demotivational

A female policeperson accompanied a male policeperson. Sexist. A male policeperson accompanied a female policeperson. Sexist. A male and a female, both policepersons (policepeople?) showed up together at precisely the same time to look into the incident of apparent vandalism at the university. Vandalism had occurred, this they deduced immediately. The lab where the policepeople stood looking at the vandalism, 7-14, was the only laboratory in the university that had been vandalised. From this they deduced that the vandals either got bored after hitting one laboratory, or they had a vendetta against the people in the lab or that ran it, or they were after a piece of research. Having met Doctor Barta Savage for all of 18 seconds the policepersons agreed amongst themselves that Vendetta was a strong possibility – the woman seemed like the type to attract enemies. They didn't rule out the Boredom or Espionage theories, but Vendetta became the working one.

Veronica Dempsey was in a pickle having a bit of a dilemma. She wanted to know who was responsible for messing up her tidy experiments, so she should be completely truthful to aid the enquiry. Conversely she was a fugitive and couldn't let on to the fact. Oh, what to do! She knew she couldn't tell them about her work in case they realised she had illegally not reported the death of a body and even more illegally got rid of it.

Social interactions with Veronica (is she retarded or just dumb?) Dempsey were strained at best. A typical greeting might proceed along the lines of:

'Morning Veronica, how are you this fine day?'

With a typical response along the lines of, 'Yes.'

Ah, to hell with it. Like questioning Veronica Dempsey about the mess was going to make any difference. She didn't know anything pertinent; therefore it was no big thing to lie. Veronica decided to use her Superior Intellect to avoid telling the truth to the male and female (equally ranked) policefuzz. Sort of like a game.

'Hi Veronica,' the female said, almost as if she was in charge (that statement is without prejudice), 'how are you today?'

'Yes,' Veronica said.

The fuzz people looked at each other.

'How are you today?' The female fuzz repeated.

'Yes,' Veronica repeated.

'Are you doing okay?' PC Woman tried.

'Ah,' Veronica said and then remained quiet.

'A bit shaken up?'

'Have you seen the mess?' Veronica countered with.

'Can you tell me what you do here?'

It was crunch time. Time to lie to an official. Time to see where the cards would settle. Time to play.

'My research focuses on activation energy barriers surrounding the Friedel-Crafts alkylation type reactions *et al.*' She finished with a satisfactory smile and italicised speech.

'Can you think of anyone that might be interested in your work?'

'What, the Ea of F-Cs? Shouldn't really think so, mate. It's derivative and without application to the world.' Good response, Veronica, very cool, nicely played.

'Thanks for your time,' PC Man said and shooed her out.

The police partners of equal rank and pay got distressed smiles from Pauline Burns and strange innuendo from Davey Jones.

'What a terrible catastrophe,' Pauline Burns had said, trying not to break into her default facial expression of a toothy grin. She came off as suspicious for it. She was asked if she knew of anyone with a grudge against the people in her lab, she laughed in a suspicious manner and then frowned with a smile.

'At least it brought the three of us together,' Davey Jones had said, meaning himself and his two female fellow lab mates who were all going through the hardship in a consolidatory way. The PCs thought 'the three of us' referred to the both of them and Davey Jones, almost as if he had an unconscious psychological desire to be on the police radar. The boy was suspicious.

Doc Barta Savage probably hadn't ransacked her own laboratory, but she was definitely suspicious.

'Let's arrest them all,' PC Male said, in a not very PC way, 'they're a bunch of chemicalist weirdos.'

'No,' PC Female said, 'do you know how to make shampoo? We need them.'

'Which one said they make shampoo?' the PC Male said.

'I'll arrest you for being dense,' the PC Female said, 'none of them specifically, but that's what chemicalists do in general.'

They decided to call a day at that, all notes were taken, all employees interviewed and moved from the Employee File to the Suspicious File, so the police humanoids went home. A job well done by all.

Veronica was dead wrong in her analysis of the situation. By not mentioning her secret line of research the cops didn't have the proverbial snowball's chance in a real hell of solving the crime. It was all about her magenta opium.

Two nights later the lab was hit again. This one was done by stealth, not a bad tempered Peter O'Shaughnessy, for it was he and he alone that had ransacked the lab on the first occasion with sandwiches and breaking glass. No, no, this time it was sly, it was sneaky, it had been done with such stealth it could have been done by aliens; in and out, no sign of anything out of place. Only Veronica noticed someone had rifled. She knew the cleaners' routines and habits; she knew the method in their seemingly random movement of her well placed objects as they cleaned. Within the lab, that is, she was not privy to their less than moral shenanigans on the eighth floor. Someone had rifled and then tried to pretend they hadn't. Veronica kept this information to herself, stored in the strongroom of Secrets, which was getting quite full. Keeping a secret about the removal of a dead body takes up a lot more brain space than, for instance, keeping a secret about getting on a train and then getting off at the next stop without paying a fare. She wondered how many secrets she could keep squashing into her brain before they would start to seep out.

Chapter, the TwentyEighth
Not For The Faint-Hearted

What follows is an account of something that happens between two adults, both of sound mind, neither coerced, each willing participants. Skip this chapter at will.

Mr Dempsey – yes, it's that time – was happy because it was Tuesday. Tuesday was a good day. One of his special good days. Now his wife was of a known fixed abode in the jail, and no longer in the unknown fixed abode of the loft nor the known temporary abode of the loft, he had many good days, and even when the day wasn't good in a special way, they were still good days. Tuesday was a special good day.

He ate beans peppered with non-peppered hotdogs made from chicken (that's what labels are there for, reading and learning what you eat: read and learn) and his excitement grew as his time approached for his most recent bar none Gardener Street excursion. He didn't care that it should be called Gardener Grove or Gardener Crescent or Gardener Cul-De-Sac rather than Gardener Street. How many gardeners lived in it? Professionally speaking, none. Amateurly speaking, a few. Street names are not made up under oath. No one on Prince Albert Avenue has a Prince Albert. Gardener Street was Mr Dempsey's pathway to contentment and, as such, should be renamed Contentment Path, if street names were made up under oath, which they weren't, or not very many men would move to Prince Albert Avenue. Sofia Mancini was not asked by lawyers if she was a gardener when she moved in. She did not reply that she knew how to take care of her bush.

Before the special good day could become especially good at the appointed hour on Gardener Whatever, Sofia had made it a prematurely special good day for Mr Dempsey by calling at the bank in an official depositing way. She had to get rid of more of her money, which no longer fitted in her purse. Mr Dempsey basked in their secret from a distance of eight feet and safety screen between them. He was stuck serving a three hundred year old customer who wanted a subscription to AirFix Magazine – 'AirFix magazine, like the soldiers boy, yes. I fought in the war. What's a sort code?' – but he was content enough in his secret with the spectacular woman to enjoying the premature basking. She allowed him to bask. She quietly encouraged it by smiling at him from eight feet and a safety screen away. Before she left she gave him a slow wink. He was one of her favourites, along with all the rest.

He arrived for his Appointment For Contentment at the appointed time and within a minute stood as naked as a French Nudist Beach and as unashamed.

'Good lad,' Sofia said as she pinned a towel round his bare ass, nappy style, 'do you want to play?'

No comment shall be made in this commentary of the events on Gardener Street as to the motive behind Mr Dempsey's motives. Speculation can be drawn over his relationship with his mother, his estranged and strange wife and his super sperm, but the workings of Mr Dempsey's mind belong to Mr Dempsey alone. Sofia didn't try to understand any of her favourite sub's motives – and they were all her favourites. No judgement shall be made on the events; Sofia never judged. She brought him a selection of children's toys; coloured building blocks, a train with Sesame Street (is it a Street? Where does it lead?) characters on it that lit up when pushed and a soft football made of foam rubber, once a green colour, now grey like a soldier's soul.

'What shall we play with first?' she asked.

He pointed to the ball.

'The ball?' she coaxed.

He nodded.

'Can you use your big boy words?'

He petted his lip: she didn't judge him.

'Okay,' she said, 'let's play!'

He played a role. She played a role. He rolled the ball to her, unjudged. She rolled it back, unjudging. They made a square with their legs, feet touching feet, legs splayed. Rolling the ball, rolling their time there. More rolling. More rolling. Till he became whiny. She didn't raise a hand to him, just asked, 'Are you finished with the ball? What would you like now?'

He pointed at the blocks.

'Block,' she said, 'blo-ck. Blo-ck.'

'Bok,' he said.

'Good lad,' she said, never tiring of never judging.

She lined the blocks up in front of him and he built a tower of three. He tried to put a fourth on top and it toppled over. He whined. He was one of her favourites.

'Oh, that was a good effort! Try again,' she said.

He built four and whined again. His role was harder to maintain than hers. He had deferred his ultimate pleasure as long as he could stand. The role was slipping. Every time he tried to keep it going for longer, he wanted to wait, to show her he could wait, to have more control. He whined.

'Are you fed up with the blocks already?' she laughed, 'How about building me a yellow tower? Just yellow blocks. Amarillo.'

His stomach sighed in disappointment. His role was almost out of grip. He built a yellow tower of seven with no daylight in between.

'Good lad!' she said, she believed in positive language for her favourites. 'Are you hungry?'

'*Thanks be to Jesus!*' he thought. At last!

She sat on the sofa and he climbed up beside her. At last. At last! His heart was thrown around his ribcage like a ping-pong ball in a tumble drier. At last! She opened her blouse. *Thank you Jesus!* She released the flap of her nursing bra exposing a large milky globe – at long last! His heart calmed to a panic as he suckled onto her nipple and fed off her. She was sweet and sticky and so warm. His body relaxed in bliss as the woman's nectar oozed down his throat, warming him from the inside. While at her breast he literally didn't have a care in the world. She didn't judge him. He gave her the power and she maintained it in a judgeless way. Half way through feeding she stopped and burped him. He finished feeding on her other side where she was sweeter and stickier and oh, so much warmer. *Praise be to Jesus for this woman!*

After the food that satisfied more than food he soiled his nappy – still she didn't judge him. She cleaned him up (non judgementally, like that even needs to be stated at this point) and suddenly – for it was always suddenly for him – their time was up. He dressed himself and left with a contentment in his belly that nothing else in the world could match.

Chapter, the TwentyNinth
Conversations With Villains

Life in the laboratory on floor 7, room 14 returned to a working normal following the Vandalism Incident. The Cops had already closed the case without suspects and a desire to never have to deal with chemicalists again. Davey Jones and Pauline Burns talked often of that "exciting night" when their lab was "torn apart" in a "vandalous act" and posed the question, 'What if we'd been working late? We could have been killed!' Their shared near death experience brought them closer. Unfortunately for Davey Jones – who still had designs on both his co-working females (literally, he had drawn up technical specifications on them) – the 'if we were here when the lab was destroyed' was too big an if for Pauline Burns to put out for him, to use American euphemism. They never worked late so it was an if that would never happen. The Impossible If. Like, 'if I had superpowers I would sell my service to the highest bidder', as opposed to The Possible If. Like, 'if I get home from work early I'll have a bath'. She hadn't come close enough to death to be that desperate to do something that stupid. She couldn't smell her death. But she played along with the bravado talk about how they could have been heroes, had they worked all night that night because she got to show off her Ultraviolet Catastrophe Teeth a lot.

'I could have tripped him up and you could have poured acid in his eyes, thus disabling him from killing us,' Davey Jones said.

'Yeah, or we could have thrown liquid nitrogen on him and frozen him for the police,' Pauline Burns chipped in.

'Or hit him with the mallet, shattering him into a billion pieces, like they do in that Terminator movie,' Davey Jones added[9].

'They do that in a James Bond movie too,' Pauline Burns said[10].

'It must work then,' Davey Jones said absently, his mind had already wandered to a James Bond scenario where he had saved the girls by freezing and smashing the villain and was just about to get thanked James Bond girl-style by both Pauline and Veronica when it occurred to him he hadn't seen Veronica that day.

'Is Veronica off?' He asked Pauline.

'That's weird,' she said, 'she's never off.'

'Maybe she got kidnapped by the vandal,' Davey Jones laughed. Pauline Burns laughed.

Meanwhile across town Veronica Dempsey was not laughing. She wasn't laughing because she was unable to get into work that day because she had been kidnapped. Not by the messy vandalising Peter O'Shaughnessy that everyone knew had vandalised the lab (not by name, naturally), but by the second person to violate the laboratory, the one who did it with so much stealth nobody even knew he'd been there. No one but Veronica, that is, who knew the alignment of her work was wrong. Veronica Dempsey's mind was irritated: her right hand bindings were tighter than her left. She twisted her left hand, trying to equal the pressure on each

---

[9] The Terminator movie to which he refers is Terminator 2 – Judgement Day: ASIN B0028U0CFS. It's alright, like. A nice twist on the Arnie character from the first movie. James Cameron again takes the helm, so it is visually top notch, even if the characters appear slightly two-dimensional.

[10] The Bond movie to which she refers is Goldeneye, Pierce Brosnan's first attempt at playing the suavely less misogynistic 007. Directed by Martin Campbell this is a good attempt by all ... if you like that sort of thing ... The relevant ASIN is B001EINT5U.

hand. There was too much blood in her left hand. Her right hand was dying at a faster rate. Her left hand had too much vitality. Her feet were equally bound, but too loose for her liking. She should feel it constraining the passage of oxygen. Her feet bindings were a ham. They were a show. They annoyed her, but without irritating her brain. Her left hand cooled; it was working. Her mind was working too fast: even the flow of blood, need to get to university, have to take off reaction, have to put on reaction, have to eat lunch, have to renew biodegrading bathtub on Sunday, must keep to schedule, drugs to make, bodies to make disappear, Proctor won't know what to do.

'Can you tighten my left wrist?' Veronica asked the figure in the shadows. He stayed away.

'Can I go now?' she asked instead. He hadn't shown his face so she couldn't see why he would object; she couldn't identify him in a line up even if she had the inclination.

'I haven't asked you anything yet,' he said.

'Can I go soon, please?'

He ignored her, 'Where are your lab notes?'

'In my lab, you must have seen them,' she said.

'What do you mean?'

'You were in my lab,' there was neither question nor accusation in her tone.

'No I wasn't,' he said defensively.

'Yes you were,' she said.

'No I wasn't,' he repeated.

'The odds of you smelling like deuterated cyclohexane and reagent grade dichloromethane and metallated isoprene by chance are astronomically high, when all three were on my bench. But I also detect some potassium hydroxide, so you also had a cursory look over the other benches.'

'I don't smell,' he said even more defensively.

'You have lots of smells; your head smells of old skin, your body smells of aerosol, your pants smell of piperidine, your feet smell of baby powder mixed with sweat and your hands smell of deuterated cyclohexane, reagent grade dichloromethane, metallated isoprene, a touch of KOH and unscented soap.'

He sniffed his hands. 'I do not smell,' he repeated, his voice at DEFCON 1. He sniffed his hands again. Nothing. 'How can you smell those things?'

'I smell like a shark,' she said.

'What does a shark smell like?'

'Fishy,' she laughed hysterically for the first time in her life at the first joke she had ever told in her life. Tears streamed down her face as she replayed the joke, 'what does a shark smell like?', 'fishy!'

'What's happening?' She asked. She laughed till breathing was difficult. After ten solid minutes she stopped laughing and said, 'That was interesting. Can I go now?'

He wanted to say yes. Some battles were lost from the start, like telling the tide not to come in. If you get to the beach at just the right time it might appear as though the tide is doing your bidding, but it never will. The moon is too cruel a mistress for the tide to ever disobey, even for a lark. The tide will always come back to the shore. He wasn't going to get anywhere with her. She was just a girl doing a bit of research. There were no military applications from her work, she wasn't going to unleash World War Three and she was hardly likely to become an evil mastermind. He suddenly felt strong compassion towards her, like the "special" daughter he never had. He couldn't treat her like a criminal, she wasn't a criminal. He couldn't treat her like a suspected terrorist, she wasn't a suspected terrorist. He let her go, knowing she wouldn't cause any trouble – she didn't. She wouldn't go to the police – she didn't. She would lie about how she spent the morning – she did.

'I had the dentist,' she told the others in lab 7-14, all the while squishing 'Got Kidnapped' into her Secrets Strongroom of her Mind. Davey Jones took an icepack from the freezer and sellotaped it to his leg. Pauline Burns buzzed to her hive. It was business as normal in 7-14.

Chapter, the Thirtieth
When Worlds Collide

Suddenly, and without a fanfare, Jessica Dempsey was released from prison. No one remembered she was getting out, no one met her at the gates. She sighed. The previous few weeks had been difficult for her; her unshakable self-belief had been shaken. No individual event triggered the shaking, but her time incarcerated wore on her brain, ebbing away at her view of the world, slowly eroding her foundations. No one met her at the gates. Quite right. She didn't deserve it. She had behaved poorly towards her family, she saw that. She had made what could easily be construed as selfish choices. She had been forced into them, of course, it hadn't been her fault. It was the internet. The internet had been her destruction; prison, her salvation. The internet was the reason she had run off and the reason she had become a bit of a slut. The Cougar Society had rejected her membership application for the very reason she was too much of a slut. Because of the internet she knew what a Cougar was when referring to a woman. Because of the internet enlightenment about what a Cougar was when referring to a woman she was also aware it had an older meaning, one that meant a big cat. She also now had a fair idea what disambiguation meant. A Cougar is a woman of age and means who likes to date younger men. Jessica Dempsey decided that when she left prison she would date younger men. However, no manner of new words learned from Wikipedia could make up for all the heartache the internet had caused her. Before her interpium addiction she would never have become a criminal nor someone who lets her tits out her bra for money. Damn internet.

Thus, in her closing weeks in lock-up she came to the realisation that the internet was an evil tempter and the downfall of her emotional wellbeing and her standing within society. The realisation brewed and bubbled and frothed until it became full scale anger. She found it difficult to be angry at the internet, it was like being angry at clouds; completely pointless (damn clouds). She couldn't hurt the internet. Yet the anger continued to brew, bubble and froth until it became delirium. Someone had to pay. Bill Gates? Unlikely. Steve Jobs? If only, but she was a PC. And he was no longer hurtable, may he RIP. The Babbages? If she had a time machine, maybe. Pete, the Firm Buttocked. Abso-fragging-lutely.

As she had nowhere else to go, Jessica Free At Last Dempsey went to the house she called home. It was a Friday afternoon; her husband, soon to be ex now she had Cougar aspirations, would be at work; Veronica would be at university (a solid assumption, but only correct now it was post meridiem and she had been released from her brief captivity of the ante meridiem) and Proctor at an unknown location. She lay down on her marital bed. It was comfortable but had the wrong smell. She didn't exist in that life any more. The loft knew she would be back today but didn't meet her at the prison gates; the loft didn't forget, the loft waited for her inevitable visit. C'mon in, defile me some more, why don't you?

As Chance would have it the loft was currently entertaining another guest. A stranger had arrived quite unexpectedly for a snoop. That hadn't ended well for the last snooper, whose current abode was a steel bath in the West Country, for about 40% of him, the other 60% spread across the waste water treatment system. Fortunately and thankfully, this stranger was not going to accidentally murder himself with an overdose of pretty pink deadly sherbet powder as Veronica Dempsey had subsequently removed all lab equipment and illegally beautiful substances. That didn't mean the loft was going to be lenient. (The loft objects again! Point of law – the loft commits no heinous crimes! It is not complicit!) The stranger heard the door and froze in the loft: his recon mission said that the male senior would be at work, the female minor would be at university and the male minor no longer visited. No female senior appeared during the recon visits and the possibility of one existing and being a threat was discounted from the decision to search the house in the middle of a Friday afternoon. The stranger waited and listened. Pottering about was happening. The loft, not one to back away from a good confrontation, whispered to Jessica, calling her, tempting her, annoying her till she got off the bed and made her way up to the second and a half floor. The Snooping Stranger tried to meld into the walls. Jessica opened the hatch, the sound was soothingly familiar. The loft smelled weird though. It smelled wrong. All wrong. In her day it smelled of lasers and computer casings and stale duvets and secrecy. There were traces of chemicals, she didn't know their names or their purpose, or why they were invading her nose. She wanted to smell lasers. It wasn't her refuge any longer. In amongst the new foreign smells there was a smell she knew, an undertone, very subtle. Her neurons fired madly. There were very few traits Veronica Genetic Throwback Dempsey got from her mother, the Ex-Con, but her smelling ability was one. They were the most expert smelling humans that God had ever made. Jessica's brain did the computation, it matched nasal stimulus with appropriate memory function.

'Hello, Pete,' she said.

Chapter, the ThirtyFirst
From A Whisper…

Ponds smell like roof tiles. Stones smell cold in the winter and warm in the summer. Blood smells of more than iron; it smells like syrup. Angel Delight smells like toothache. Argon smells like pot pourri made from shards of mixed metals. Potassium smells like bananas. Crispy Duck with beanshoots smells of zinc. The Dempsey females were each unaware that the other had the same keen sense of smell. They weren't able to smell over greater distances than the average nose, they were simply able to differentiate smells at almost the atomic level. Pirelli tyres smelled different from Dunlop tyres. Pink garden slabs smelled different from white garden slabs. Bricks on the sunrise wall of the house smelled different from bricks on the west side.

Jessica Dempsey, like her daughter Veronica Smells Like A Shark (But Not Fishy, Ha Ha) Dempsey, never forgot a smell. Firm_Buttock_Pete was, for whatever Godforsaken reason, hiding out in her loft, snooping around in her loft, hanging out in her loft, being in her loft. He was moving towards her from behind, without sound but not without aroma. His smell stimulated more nerve endings in her nose: he was getting closer. He was sneaking, with intent. He was going to attack; there was no other reason for his lack of greeting following hers and his attempt at stealth. 'He's going to attack me,' she thought just as he lunged at her rear. She moved out the way, swinging her bag towards his head. She made a sterling contact and he was knocked out cold. A moment later he was bleeding stealthily into the carpet.

Not another one! One death in the loft might be considered misfortune, but two is downright carelessness! The loft objects, like it makes any difference. People keep coming to die in the loft, not at the loft's request, no. In spite of the loft's good character. Upstanding character! It's a conspiracy. The loft listed how a conspiracy against it could start: the tumble dryer, too easily hot and bothered and undersized and fractious and decidedly murderous; the neighbourhood swarm of cats, always up to no good; the greenhouse, ah, that's a very likely candidate. The greenhouse and the loft once shared something special, something beyond magical, but the greenhouse changed, it wanted –

The corpse groaned.

Oh, thank the Maker! This one wasn't dead. Maybe it wasn't a conspiracy after all, but nonetheless the greenhouse was on the radar. Aye.

Jessica hit him again and he passed out again. While he was unconscious this time she went to find something to tie him up, which was more difficult than she imagined. If they were gardening people she might have had cable ties, but they weren't, so she didn't. If they were outdoorsy people she might have had rope, but they weren't, so she didn't. If they were DIY people she might have had duct tape, but they weren't, so she didn't. They were normal (after a fashion) people with normal things. They had dental floss in the bathroom; too flimsy. They had spaghetti in the kitchen; too brittle. They had figurines in the lounge; too figurine-like. She found a roll of sellotape. It was going to have to do. She wrapped his wrists behind his back with approximately 130 layers of tape. She did the same with his ankles. She then sellotaped his bound wrists to his bound ankles with approximately 390 layers of tape. That should hold him for a little while. Time was not good. It was making her eyes pruney and her arms saggy, but the more urgent concern over time was that it was almost time for her husband (soon to be ex, even sooner if he found out she had a randomer bound and gagged – oh yeah, better gag him – in the loft. That was a step beyond pirating in the loft) to come home. She knew how to survive for a weekend in the loft undetected, she had done it 434 times, give or take, in her voluntary exile for 8 years, 4 months and 18 days there. But she needed supplies. It was going to be tight, but she had enough "time" to go to the Co-Op – I wonder if they sell cable ties? – and back before the rest of the Dempseys arrived home on a regular Friday afternoon. Firm_Buttock_Pete was breathing and bleeding. She sellotaped a wad of toilet roll onto his head and another over his mouth. Sorted. Unconscious, gagged, bandaged and sellotaped he looked precisely like he was being kidnapped by a mental. There's no such thing as coincidence.

The Co-Op had food and water and cat litter and alcohol and pastries and greeting cards and toileteries, exactly the sorts of things that smallish local shops sell, but it didn't have survival knives, knuckle dusters, industrial strength cable nor chloroform, exactly the sort of things smallish local shops don't sell. She bought a selection of normal things that the Co-Op did sell. On the way home she popped into a hardware-cum-haberdashery-cum-army surplus store where she bought cable ties, duct tape and a BB gun that looked like a normal gun. Worried that it might come across suspiciously like she had a stranger kidnapped in her loft she also bought an ironing board cover, an Action Man and a hostess trolley. She got home with "no time" to spare. Getting the hostess trolley up vertical ladders into the loft was a bit of a struggle, but in her 8 year, 4 month and 18 day holiday up there she had managed to get a bed in there, so she pulled it off, relying heavily on her good teeth. There was just enough "time" to put cable ties on the still unconscious Snooper and swap the sellotaped mouth for a duct taped one just as he woke up and just as

Mr Dempsey unlocked the front door. It was going to feel like a very long weekend till she could leave the loft again, and that fact weighed on nothing more heavily than the loft itself.

Chapter, the ThirtySecond
Sunday. Bleeding Sunday

Sunday. Bleeding Sunday.
  Sunday. Bleeding Sunday.
  The trips to the West Country were becoming a bit of a bore. Mordor grew gloomier; Brigadoon, blah; the Styx was pretty the first couple of times but once you've seen the entrance to the underworld once you've seen it as many times as you need to until you finally need to and pay to ride it, plus it really stank; Atlantis was samey and the Islets of Langerhan were old hat. Admittedly the Seven Seas of Rhye didn't depreciate with subsequent viewings, it rocked every time. But when one must get rid of a body one must make sure the body is well and truly gotten rid of. If a job's worth doing, it's worth doing well: never has a trite corporate statement been more apt. The phrase itself was probably coined for disposing of illegally dead bodies. There was the added complication on this trip of Veronica Dempsey wondering if she would be getting followed. Two days previously she had been kidnapped for a few hours by one of the people to raid the lab. Two parties had raided the lab, and the party responsible for her kidnapping was not Peter O'Shaughnessy. Peter O'Shaughnessy had no alibi for the morning of the kidnapping, being alone in the Dempsey household, where he still remained having been ab-

ducted himself in a stroke of severe bad luck. He was still to be found, if anyone went looking, under the Dempsey roof but above the living floors wondering why he was being held hostage.

If someone was to go to all the trouble of breaking into the lab and then the even more trouble of kidnapping Veronica (and not getting himself kidnapped in the process) she concluded it wasn't too much of a stretch of the brain cells to assume he might be trailing her. But let's not forget he had broken into her lab and kidnapped her, both illegal activities, so who was he to judge her for her illegal Country Cottage Decomposing Man? When sin stones were to be thrown he would not be casting the first one. Should she even care if he found out? She texted Proctor for advice:

Hi, got kidnapped a bit on Friday, might be getting followed, will we be okay for Sunday?

Proctor's reply was short:

Fine will pick u up a hour earlier. (sic)

He didn't waste his time asking her to clarify how she could be "kidnapped a bit", he'd find out soon enough. Leaving an hour earlier suited him well, it meant he'd have an extra hour with his Butterfly Goddess.

Off they set, an hour before stupid o'clock and alert to anyone acting more suspiciously than them. There was no one. For who could be more suspicious than a pair of siblings (a modest-to-poorly tattooed male and a milky-skinned-average female), awake before the moon said goodnight, driving erratically, stopping, pausing, passing, creeping, looking all around, before embarking on a land cruise past Mordor, by Brigadoon, over the Styx, skimming past Atlantis, flirting with the road to the Islets of Langerhans and beyond the Seven Seas of Rhye, arriving at a destination undefined save to say "the West Country" and "Steel Bath" to visit the remains of a Pointy Toothed (but not for religious or ceremonial grounds, that has been explicitly delineated) Decomposing at an Acceptably Accelerated Rate P.I.? There was Mr Francois, sneaking home after spending the night surreptitiously counting all the security cameras in town and calculating their field of vision. Not suspicious enough to compete with the Double Dempseys. How about Ms Sandyford? She arrived home every morning an hour before stupid o'clock having spent the evening on her reverse counting stars and raindrops. Her hair was unkempt in a hugely suspicious manner, but nowhere close to the DD pair. In short, and as iterated already, in the search for people acting more suspiciously than them, there were none. Proctor took the long way out of town stopping at lots of traffic lights to be sure no one was following and set off, once again, to visit the remains of Mr D. Ville.

'No washing powder today?' Proctor asked.

'Nope, phase two.'

All the skin and muscle had non-magically non-mysteriously, just science in practice, disappeared over the course of a few weeks, eaten by the special enzymes in modern washing powder specifically engineered to eat away at stubborn stains and even more stubborn flesh. The once well upholstered flesh was now unupholstered. All that was left of the illfortunate spy were his yellowing bones, which Veronica took from the bath and towel dried. The leg and arm bones were big and easy to handle, but the smaller bones – there are hundreds of the things! – she scooped out of the bath by the handful. Once everything was dabbed with the conveniently supplied cotton polyester blend towels she took the Calcium-rich remains of the body to the kitchen and packed them all into the oven, like a macabre game of Tetris. That bit was quite fun. The leg bone was connected to a rib bone. That rib bone was connected to several spine bones. Those spine bones were connected to many phalanges. The oven was set to 230 degrees C, lit, and she left. Over 500 Kelvin should do it.

'Sorted?' Proctor asked when she got back into the car.

'Phase two,' she replied. She had hired the picturesque cottage for a few extra weeks.

They got home in jig time, the rainbow road fairly clear of traffic. Veronica Dempsey was pleased with how well Operation D. Ville Disposal was going; the flesh and squishy bits were all at sea and the bones were drying out professionally. Proctor Dempsey was pleased it was almost over. Every time they made the journey was a risk that he'd end up in jail again, separated from his Sofia, from his oxygen, from his protein supply and Butterfly; every time he didn't it was an energy rush to have her back again.

Jessica Dempsey, holed up in the loft just like old times (although in olden times she had a bed and the internet, this time all she had was a hostage and a hostess trolley), was pleased with how distraught Firm_Buttocked_Loose_Stooled_Pete was. The universe had sent him to her for retribution, what other reason would there be for him being in her loft? None whatsoever. He was a gift from the Goddess of Justice. Vengeance was hers to take on this creature that used her shamelessly and forced her into a life of internet slutdom and piracy. He had wronged her. It was all his fault. It was no coincidence that Fate brought them together. Fate wanted her to kill him.

Peter O'Shaughnessy lost all sense of time. He tried to sleep as much as possible. His head was warm and crusty. His limbs were numb and cold. His captor drank water sparingly and peed into a bucket. He occasionally peed his trousers and she sprayed him with Febreeze.

'Oh my God,' Peter O'Shaughnessy thought every time he was conscious, 'this mad fucker is going to kill me.'

Chapter, the ThirtyThird
Love Is A Verb

While driving through Mordor (gloomy!), by Brigadoon (blah!), over the Styx (been there, done that stinky thing!), past Atlantis (it's just so samey!), beside the Islets of Langerhans (so old hat!), along the Seven Seas of Rhye (ooh, pretty!), Proctor Dempsey could no longer fantasize about ringing the doorbell of the mysterious woman with the butterfly tattoos, because that was in the past. His few weeks with Sofia had become his entire life; everything that came before was blurred in an amniotic fluid haze. He wasn't scared of being near train tracks, but his lack of suicidal tendencies was just a part of the revelation about what his life should be. She introduced him to Thai food's subtle flavours, to Japanese movies' passionate cinematography and awakened every stimulus in his body for sex. She was beyond anything this earth could produce. Her protons were formed from adventure, her electrons powered by eroticism and her neurons, they were what happy is made of.

He made a decision. His track record was shoddy in that department, but then, he didn't come from good stock: his dad … his dad cannot be mentioned because it brings his mind back to what his dad does with Sofia, and Proctor Dempsey is unable to give that a single thought; his mother was, at the very moment he made his decision, holed up in the loft with a cable-tied, duct-taped intruder (not her best decision, and not thought out), and Veronica was into some weird tripping powder, possibly murder, and at the very least had decided to hide a death from the police, something they didn't particularly like happening. His previous track record of decision making resulted in a miserable life and a spell in jail. Nonetheless he made a decision, and he was happy.

He dropped Veronica at home, her dastardly deed complete for another week and drove to his bedsit. Sofia was already there. Sunday was their special day. She didn't ask where he spent his mornings. She wasn't the jealous type; even if he did have a mistress as long as he had enough energy for her she didn't care. Even if he knew that she wouldn't care if he took a mistress he never would, but he'd love her all the more for it. Even if she knew that he was driving his sister to decompose the body of a snooping private investigator in the West Country she wouldn't care. If he knew that she wouldn't care if she knew that he was driving his sister to the West Country to decompose the body of a snooping private investigator he'd love her all the more for it.

He wasted no time. He had decided. She was there, glowing with ethereal energy from her quarks out. He got down on one knee and asked her to marry him.

If there are an infinite number of alternate universes, and she said yes in half of them, then she said yes an infinite amount of times in other existences. She also said no in an infinite number of universes. But in an infinite number of universes he never asked her. In an infinite number of universes Proctor Dempsey and Sofia Mancini have never met. In an infinite number of universes Proctor Dempsey doesn't exist. In an infinite number of universes Sofia Mancini doesn't exist. In an infinite number of universes mankind has learned the ability to fly. In an infinite number of universes there is no life on Earth. In an infinite number of universes there is no Earth. In an infinite number of universes there are no universes. Our existence, one of an infinite number of existences

– infinity to the power infinity! – is so statistically irrelevant we don't even exist. This is why infinities should never be bandied about. It is more than a word, it's a belief system, requiring more faith than reincarnation, evolution and Scientology combined.

Assuming we do exist, and assuming this book exists (as it does in an infinite number of universes, both the version you hold and an infinite number of other versions), then the Sofia Mancini, daughter of a Mobster, Dominatrix, Sex Goddess and all round Loveable Dudette, smiled sweetly at Proctor Dempsey, offspring of a Harmless Pervert and a Dangerous Pervert, Ex-Con, Tattooed Dude and all round Good Guy To Have In A Death In The Loft Emergency Scenario, and said, 'Sure.' She meant it too. She was sure.

'Let's get a penguin as a wedding present. We'll call him Frederick on Sundays and Freddie the rest of the week. I don't mind if he can't dance, we'll still love him. Or her. She can be Freddie as well and Fredericka on a Sunday. Every new couple should have a penguin. We'll eat shrimp vol-au-vents and drink Chardonnay together and watch a flatscreen television and Freddie will hug me while you're out at work.'

They sealed the deal with some funky sex followed by dinner at Luigi and Maria's house, where they broke the good news.

'We're getting married,' Sofia said over the store-bought (and delicious) dessert.

'Who?' Luigi asked.

'Me and Proctor,' Sofia said patiently.

Maria cried. Possibly from happiness; she never expected to see her daughter in a wedding dress. Possibly from awkwardness; what names would go on the wedding invitations? Would it be official if they used their assumed names of Luigi and Maria? Possibly from guilt; once again she had been unable to prepare a decent dessert and had bought one in. What sort of fake Italian mama cannot make dessert? Knowing your limitations is all well and good, but why couldn't she conquer this one little thing? One good dessert, that's all she asked! Maybe all she needed was the correct motivation.

'I'm so happy!' she declared, solving the mystery of the source of the tears, 'Can I make the wedding cake?' she added, demonstrating that the tear thing may have been too quickly assigned fully to happiness, when there was also some guilt at play.

'Sure,' Sofia said. Maybe they would be alive in one of the infinite number of universes where Maria would make a successful cake (if only it could be part of the infinite number of universes where mankind had bona-fide superpowers), although the infinite number of universes where she screwed it up was probably a bigger infinity.

Chapter, the ThirtyFourth
Fate's a Bitch

Several weeks are about to pass: the research into the Opium with the Magenta solution is about to conclude at the chemical laboratory level and be handed over to drug development; Sofia and Proctor are to continue with their wedding plans, the big day set one month after the accepted proposal and close to where the story will be picked up; Doctor Barta Savage has been networking and emailing behind the scenes and polishing her Nobel Prize winning acceptance speech (not that the speech is Nobel Prize worthy, the other way to read that sentence), along with various other events. But before the weeks shall pass without comment the issue of Jessica Kidnapping Dempsey and Peter Scared Shitless O'Shaughnessy must be dealt with.

Monday morning came at last and not an instant too soon for Jessica (boy would she go straight back to jail for this one!) Dempsey, Peter (I'm gonna die, I'm gonna die, I'm gonna die) O'Shaughnessy and the loft alike. As soon as the officially domiciled Dempseys left for work and university, Jessica went downstairs to stretch her legs and make a nice cup of tea. Although she'd had all weekend to think about how to handle the looming situation, she hadn't given it any thought. She now regretted spending the weekend fantasizing about men half her age (plus seven years, as is the accepted rule) and not planning how to defuse the situation of a burly man tied up in the loft who she would have to untie and who would be fairly pissed off. She made two cups of tea.

'I'm going to take off your gag,' she told Pete when she went back up. 'You can yell, but don't scream.'

He yelled.

'Now,' she said matter-of-factly, 'I'm not going to kill you.'

'I'm going to kill her, I'm going to kill her,' he thought.

'And you're not going to kill me,' she said.

That stumped him.

'I got out of prison on Friday,' she continued, not a word of a lie. 'I made lots of contacts in there –' not true, she didn't talk to a single inmate '– of the criminal kind.' Had she talked to anyone at all then that would have been true. They were all of the criminal variety.

She convinced him that she had made phone calls whilst downstairs ensuring that if she was suddenly unavailable to, let's say, answer her phone in the near future then they would 'take care of him' in a mafia-type way. He had no idea who she was, but she knew his name and his job and his marital set up. She also knew he liked four sugars in a cup of tea.

'The thing is,' she said whilst letting him sip his tea, 'I could leave you up here, all tied up and gagged, to slowly die.'

He choked on his tea. The mad fucker was going to kill him. There was no other way for this to end.

'No one would ever find you.'

'Do it!' Fate screamed to her.

'Don't do it!' the Loft protested. Mud sticks.

Leaving him in the loft is what Fate wanted her to do. Fate gave Firm_Buttock_Pete to her, Fate wanted him dead. But if Fate wanted him dead badly enough Fate could send an artic lorry his way, minus the brakes.

'I'm going to let you go,' she said, 'and I don't care where you go as long as you never come near my house or my family ever again.'

He nodded.

'Go home to your wife.'

He nodded again.

Well, that seemed to be that taken care of, no worries. The new and improved Jessica Dempsey kicked ass, being all dominant and threatening. She had pitched her facade to perfection and the retribution he wanted to take out on her for subjecting him to the scariest, most painful 70 hours of his life was quashed by the fear of something worse happening to him by her Con Chums. She knew too much about him. He couldn't take the chance she was bluffing. The risk was too great. She was a mental and she probably had mental friends. They'd probably cut his testicles off, given half the chance. Then make him eat them. He'd heard about mental women before. That would be that then. He'd leave without a fuss. But with both testicles attached.

He left without a fuss. Both testicles intact. Brain slightly disengaged. Arms and legs transitioning from numb to aching; numb was better, of course, because it meant no aching. Pride as squishy as mashed potato that's been through a liquidiser. Insides made of water. Bones made of rubber. Alive. Fixable. Food, water, ablutions and rest would be all he needed to be a man again. Two testicles, one penis, blood thumping. Sex. That's a good idea. Nothing like firing his hot lovin' manseed into a woman to make him feel like a man – rwar! Food first. Shower first. Water, sleep first.

That was Peter (FREE!) O'Shaughnessy's plan. It wasn't Fate's. As Peter (ALIVE!) O'Shaughnessy made his way to his car an artic lorry's brakes failed, hitting Peter (OH FU-) O'Shaughnessy with enough force to flatten a rhino. Force is equal to mass multiplied by acceleration. An artic lorry has enormous mass, it was accelerating as it hit him, he was dead before his body hit the ground. It was a small mercy.

The loft was just glad the death took place outside.

Jessica the Reformed Rabbit watched from the loft. That was unexpected. Peter the Cycling Slut represented everything that had gone wrong in her life. And now he was suddenly dead, just like that. Not by her hand, nor at the loft's behest. Fate wanted her to see his death to release her. The universe wanted her to be free from the destruction his fleeting acquaintance had brought. She could now live life on her terms. He was the reason her life was rubbish. He had gone to hell (educated guess). Her future was unwritten, uncluttered and entirely hers. She surveyed the loft with fresh eyes. Oh, no you don't, it protested. Oh, yes she did. Obviously she'd avoid any pirating activity this time, nothing that the fuzz would be interested in. Webcam was good enough for starters, meanwhile she would look in to expanding her Cougar aspirations. A new bed up here, a new laptop, or maybe a tablet. It was good to be home.

The loft despaired.

Chapter, the ThirtyFifth
The Duality of Time

Cars were sold for cash and credit. People fell over and stood back up again. Very few fell straight back down. Bookies laughed into their socks. Foreigners flocked. Muzac was played in lifts and life. Trees turned blue and animal hunters shot arrows. Trades were made. Trains were late. Companies burst. The stockmarket steadied, dipped, rose, steadied, dipped, rose, steadied. Women lunched. Women lunged. Men pumped. Dogs mated. Bank notes were gathered and burned. Set squares drew perpendicular lines. CCTV caught acts of vandalism, burglary and promiscuity. Trains arrived on time and departed late. Tides went this way and that, never by will power. Fences were built. Cancer killed. Horses ran races. Bookies laughed into their socks. Cables were laid. People were laid. People wore plaid. People didn't wear plaid. Some of the people were pleased some of the time, some of the people were pleased all of the time, all of the people were pleased some of the time, all of the people were not pleased all of the time. Trainers were hand stitched by expensive machines. Medals were won. Medals were misplaced. Fornicators died. Grass was trampled. New galaxies were photographed. Space expanded. Hydrogen bonds were broken as hair was straightened at 220 degrees Celsius. Magpies ate roadkill, in solitude and despair. Hares scraped. Fish schooled. Kids schooled. Kids bleated. Fishermen meted. Icecaps melted (controversially at election time). Cookies were baked. Bins were collected by bins made of lorries. Post was deposited onto hall floors to be sorted and shredded. Toddlers grew. Electricity was harvested. Trains chooed. Diamonds were cut to sparkle. Clothes were dried on a washing line. Sandwiches were prepared, cut and enjoyed: sandwiches on white, brown, malted, tortilla, French bread. Doctor's appointments were kept, prescriptions prescribed, pharmaceuticals made profit from sickness. Bands gigged. Beer was drunk. Marriages ended with a bang. Marriages dissolved without notice. Knots were tied. Forecasts for shipping were made; landlovers didn't get it. Neon signs stopped working and were repaired. Buildings were controlled exploded. Sand was turned into glass for windows and measuring jugs. Sand was turned into cement for mortar. Trains arrived on time and departed on time. Soap operas tried to shock. Celebrities aged. Tigers hunted. Eardrums burst under pressure. Second hands ticked, minute hands tocked, hour hands crept. Iron rusted. Ideas were formed, some put into practice, some forgotten after sleep. Sopranos sang high. Boys were circumcised. Pollen spread. Clouds formed spontaneous patterns. Strawberrys rotted. Fashion stayed the same. TV was watched, downloaded and ignored.

The Moon circled the Earth ellipsing the Sun. Clouds leaked. Bookies laughed into their socks. Gravestones sank. Old buses went to purgatory. Teenage boys swaggered. Impossible dreams went undreamt. Children learned their ABCs and their 123s. Hearts were broken. Racism happened. Expensive bags were bought. Tax was paid, avoided and dodged. Birds ate bugs. Mud slid. Movie scripts were edited. Deals were made with terrorists. Pages were folded down to keep place. Armies trained. Chocolate melted in the mouth, but not in the oven. Water found its level. Social networking sites buzzed. Comics were overlooked. Colours were invented. Mountains were climbed for glory and charity. Ties were tied. Developments were developed. Excrement was excreted.

Sexually transmitted infections were transmitted, sexually. Hairpin bends were crashed on. Workers in hi-vis jackets swore. Velcro was stuck and unstuck. Leather was treated. Secret ingredients were added to Coca-Cola. Dead mice in fields decomposed. Traffic light changed from green to amber to red to red-plus-amber to green to amber to red to red-plus-amber to green to amber ...

Sharks swam for miles pointlessly, never wondering where they were going or why. Aliens flew on by. Sun traps grew warm in the sunshine. Art was admired and derided. Dancers stretched. Cowards stayed home. Petrol was pumped into thirsty tanks. Music was downloaded. Cheeseburgers were eaten. Announcements were made over Tannoy systems. Timber was felled. Tankers carted goods from east to west by sea. Airplanes defied God. Fridges were fly-tipped. Milk was drunk to cool hot curries. Supermarkets sold almost fresh produce at discounted prices. Lip gloss was applied liberally. Roundabouts were driven around. Kidneys took care of waste. Wool was cured. Muscles respired. Aerobically. Anaerobically. Aerobically. Anaerobically. Aerobically. Anaerobically. Gossip was repeated. Metal alloyed. Mysteries were solved by the police while mysteries remained unsolved. Television stations showed repeats. Spikes jagged. People jogged. Hair was dyed red and black and yellow and brown and chestnut and green. Aeroplanes defied Nature. The earth moved twelve thousand million miles through space without anyone falling off.

In short, life in the world progressed for several weeks, unaware of the life of Veronica (where do we go from here?) Dempsey *et al*.

Chapter, the ThirtySixth
All's Well

'I'm getting married on Wednesday, remember,' Proctor Dempsey told his sister as they were halfway over the Styx en route to her West Country cottage.

'I didn't forget,' Veronica answered.

'It's just,' he paused.

'Just what?' She asked.

'I can't take you here on a Sunday any more.'

'Okay,' she replied, characteristically stoically. There was nothing else she could say. She could hardly make a fuss since he'd been so helpful to that point and she didn't want to anyway. Invaluable. If it wasn't for her brother she would have put the surprisingly dead Mr D. Ville in the neighbour's bin, hoping the council wouldn't notice until it was too late. Very risky business, that would have been. It was likely that that Sunday would be their last visit anyway; Veronica would now make sure it was. It never occurred to her to think she had gotten away with murder as the black people who had meetings inside her head, and acted as part-time jury members, were still out holding discussions on the psychological arguments for and against her being complicit in murder. She was getting away with something, that much they agreed on, then they had a tea break with caramel shortbread squares and talked about football instead.

Proctor hummed a Billy Ocean song and before they knew it they were once again at the whitewashed tomb of the cottage.

The bones had been in the full fire oven for weeks. Full fire was archaic. It was electric; the element didn't form a plasma, just heat. The electromagnetic series said no. She turned the oven off and left the door open. The bones had to be at the optimum temperature for Phase three; cool enough to touch, but warm enough to be brittle. Science in everything. Science behind everything. Science for every day life. Proctor waited in the car, as he always did, thinking about Sofia, the butterfly that had cocooned his life and taught him how to fly, as he always did. Veronica was taking longer than usual. She better not be napping in the beautiful cottage … He had an immense idea mid-thought. Veronica had the place hired till the weekend, he could bring his bride here on Wednesday night as a surprise. He looked at the cottage with fresh eyes: welcoming, rustic, friendly, old school. It would be nice to get away for their wedding night and that was a nice place. Welcoming, rustic, friendly, old school. He'd ask Veronica when she got back. She might be a murderer – who knew? – but she was still family. She'd say yes. He wondered while he was at it what she'd bought him as a wedding present. It was a snakeskin trumpet. He would never have wondered that far. Veronica Dempsey had only been to one family wedding before. She was twelve at the time and in response to the question, 'isn't the bride beautiful?' she had replied, 'no, she's as ugly and fat as she is every other day only today she looks like the Marshmallow woman.' Veronica Dempsey was promptly uninvited to all further family gatherings. She stood by her honest assessment of the situation and wasn't prepared to take a chance on going to hell for lying just because it was someone's "special day", "special" for everyone to lie to the couple and tell her she looked pretty when she didn't and tell him he married someone pretty when he didn't. What if she had died that night? She'd have gone to heaven only to be turned away by Saint Peter himself who just wouldn't listen to her excuse of 'I was told I was supposed to lie to fat, ugly brides'. 'Talk to the hand,' is what Saint Peter would say and she'd instantly be transported to hell, where she'd be poked in the eye for an eternity by a demon who looked like her cousin, the Marshmallow Bride. She was therefore unaccustomed to the etiquette of wedding present buying. A snakeskin trumpet seemed as good a gift as any, and who doesn't want a snakeskin trumpet?

The bones reached an optimum temperature for smashing, so she smashed them. Firstly she put them all in a bin bag, which she double bagged for security, then smashed them with a rolling pin. She smashed them like digestive biscuits for a cheesecake base. The surface area to volume increased as the bones got smaller and smaller. She giggled as she smashed though she didn't know why. Smashy smashing smashes of smash. Smaller pieces, bigger surface area to volume. Smashed more. Even smaller pieces, even bigger surface area to volume. The bones were done. Powdered like digestives in the base of a cheesecake. She wondered what a cheesecake would taste like if the base was made of ground up bones. The texture would probably be all wrong. Maybe shortbread made of bones would be better. She hoped the cannibals made good use of the bones; they (the bones, not the cannibals) seemed like a versatile ingredient when smashed until of a powdery constitution.

Her work at the cottage was done. She checked the bathtub: clean. She checked the oven: clean. She took her doubled-up bin bags and left the building. It had served her well in the most inconspicuous fashion, old faithful friend, not one to grass her up. Certainly disposing of the body had turned out to take quite a long time (compared to, say, making a cheesecake, not compared to rocks turning into sand), but it hadn't exactly been hard work. Done. Excellent. Good work all round, cottage and brother. Their last chore was to sprinkle the digestive biscuit bones into the Styx on the way past.

Success.

Chapter, the ThirtySeventh
Nuptially Yours

The deed was done. Success. Triumph. Ecclesiastical joy. He had got away with it. He wasn't back in jail. His mental sister had done it. Success. Beautiful success. Except ...

That night the terrors began for Proctor Dempsey. His sleep, which was usually a bout of welcome, if severe, unconsciousness, was troubled. His sleeping mind was accustomed to the peaceful sleep of the dead and now, suddenly, it was filled with intense feelings of abandonment, fear, hatred, bereavement and needing the toilet. He could never remember what he dreamt about; there were never any images to accompany the feelings, just blackness and despair. When he felt he was running away he knew he was running away from something that would undoubtedly kill him slowly to death and he felt real fear that he had never known in his waking body. His skin plummeted in temperature and he lost half a stone in sweat each night. Cold shivers and sweat.

He put it down to pre-wedding nerves, nothing at all to do with the closure of the West Country Escapades bringing the events to the forefront of his mind, no, no. Pre-wedding nerves. Everyone gets a bit jittery. It was just cold feet. His feet were very cold. Just nerves. Normal. He was Normal. Normal Proctor: No Problem. Nerves can do that to your digestion. It was just because Sofia had said they weren't spending the night together till the wedding night. She didn't stop the sex – no point cutting off her nose to spite her face – just the sleeping part. The part he clearly needed her most for. The part he was now so dependent on her for he was unable to achieve on his own. A successful night's kip without her became an impossibility. As the wedding day drew closer the fear factory of sleep intensified. Another night of it would break his brain completely. Insanity was waiting in the darkness. Insanity was testing the pressure points of his defences; probing here, prodding there, tickling yonder. One more assault and his mind would be lost forever. Insanity sniggered as it waited for him to nod off for a final time; it was ready to wrap its tentacles around his cerebral matter, squeezing and making his brain bleed ...

The bride wore burgundy. She was beyond beautiful, she was stunning. She was beyond stunning, she was effulgent. She was beyond effulgent.

The priest asked Proctor if he would look after Sofia forever, even if she gets sick, ugly and poor. Proctor replied, 'I'll take two, please, Bob.' Father Quinn's name was not Bob.

Proctor had one rule for the wedding – no "clients". Veronica Dempsey was therefore the only family member on the groom's side of the church, since Mr Dempsey was a client (the exact client Proctor didn't want at the ceremony, hence the one rule) and Mrs Dempsey was assumed still in jail and no one had bothered checking the loft recently. Veronica was coping well with an afternoon out of the lab; no hot flushes, no passing out, coping well indeed. She lied to herself and said there was a fire alarm so she couldn't be working anyway. The Wrong Order Kung Fuing Parkouring Twins were in attendance but they sat with Luigi on the bride's side, quite forgetting they were Proctor's cousins.

Whenever Proctor wasn't speaking the wedding was lovely. When he had to reply to a question or repeat his name, things became less conformist.

Father Quinn said, 'Repeat after me: I Proctor Dempsey …'

Proctor said, 'Repeat after you: You Proctor Dempsey ...'

Sofia Almost Dempsey was delighted with him. A bit of insanity in a husband was on her list of things she wanted most in a man. Proctor Dempsey didn't sleep the night before the wedding, he therefore hadn't been possessed completely by Insanity and was still borderline. Which was perfect for Sofia Now Dempsey. Sofia Effulgent In Burgundy Dempsey. Proctor cried. He had a wife. He has a wife. The most amazing woman in this or any other universe. He wouldn't swap her for any amount of money or even for Famke Jansen.

The newly weds kissed with tongues. The congregation cheered. Dinner was on fast forward for Proctor Dempsey who was suddenly exhausted once the deal was sealed with saliva. Luigi gave a speech about his how daughter did all manner of weird shit for money and that his new son-in-law was one of the best goddamn bouncers in the whole of their town. Animals also seemed to like the lad. Proctor wanted to fold himself up inside his burgundy bride and sleep for a week.

Why was everyone looking at him?

No, seriously. Why was everyone looking at him? Sofia was the main event, why waste all those lightwaves and electrical energy in the brain converting the waves into a picture on him? Couldn't they see her? She was right there, looking beyond effulgent. She was ... looking at him too. Ah crud on a stick, they all wanted some sort of speech.

'On behalf of my wife and I,' Proctor said, half rising to his feet, mustering all his energy to raise his glass, 'cheers!'

There were whistles and claps from the assembled Family.

He swigged, swallowed and sat back down again. They could look all they wanted, he was done. Sofia Dempsey was giddy. She was glad she was the exact Sofia Mancini in the exact universe that met this man and in the exact universe that married this man. The odds against it were astronomical. She was glad to be alive and to be free and to be hitched. Sometimes the universe just doesn't suck.

Chapter, the ThirtyEighth
Good For The Soul

Sometimes it does. It really does. It sucks like a bitch for a bonus. The Universe. Proctor was wrong. Wrong about Sofia. He was right about a great many things about Sofia. He was right to think he loved her. He was right to marry her. He was right to trust her, regardless of the nature of her job. He was right to consider her smarter than him. He was right to appreciate he had punched above his weight to bag her. When he thought about how the two of them belonged together, he was dead right. With respect to his depreciating brain and thinking she could save him, he was dead wrong.

   He drove her to the West Country for their wedding night as he planned. She was ecstatic with the surprise. Mordor was magnificent! Brigadoon sublime! The Styx was majestic! Atlantis spectacular! The Islets of Langerhans, tremendous! And the Seven Seas of Rhye was the most beautiful countryside she had ever laid eyes on. The cottage was quaint and the perfect ending to her eclectic day. An erotic bath in a romantic setting was all she needed for the day to be unsurpassable.

   Proctor knew something was wrong as he reached the bathroom door. Something was reaching inside his body and throwing command switches at random: his mouth dried up, his shins started sweating, his brain became itchy. The door handle stung his hand – it was freezing, at least -80 degrees. He touched it again carefully. It was normal temperature. He opened the door slowly and a rush of energy took his breath away; it swirled round him like a swarm of bees, tickling his skin but always threatening to sting every inch of him. Mr D. Ville's corpse was slumped there in the bath, exactly where Proctor had placed it weeks earlier. What the hell? Had Veronica done nothing all those times she made him drive her here? He had stayed in the car during her subsequent visits, were they all a charade? The dead man suddenly sat straight up, looked at Proctor through glassy eyes and hissed, 'You have to sleep sometime!'

'Who was that?' Sofia Free Dempsey asked.

Proctor had two choices. He could tell the woman who had just agreed to be his lifelong companion that he had assisted in the disposal of a body, not all that well since it was still in the bathroom. Or he could lie, quite easily with a 'who was what?'

He told her the truth.

He told her about his weekly vigils. She was impressed; that was much better use of his time than having an affair.

'You mean to tell me that you and your sister have been disappearing here every Sunday in a religious fashion to get rid of a dead body and you thought that would be the perfect place to take your new wife to celebrate getting married?'

'Yes,' Proctor said. Her summing up was factually correct.

'I love you,' she told him again and consummated his brains out.

Proctor was never bothered again with apparitions and demons tormenting his sleep. Turns out having a glitch in your conscience can have severe psychological effects – who knew? Proctor didn't need Sofia to calm his brain, Proctor needed release from the secret he was keeping from his new wife. The idea of hiding such a thing from her could have driven him insane. Having never had a wife before he had no idea how deep the bonds went so suddenly. Who knew?

*

After the wedding dinner Veronica Dempsey went back to the lab. The pretend fire that kept her away would have been dealt with by the efficient pretend fire brigade and she couldn't stay away any longer. She signed in at security as it was well after hours and moseyed on to the lab. Sofia had liked the snakeskin trumpet from her quirky sister-in-law and had squeezed her boobs into Veronica when she hugged her to say thank you. Veronica had liked the squishy feel of them. Maybe she was a bit gay. Perhaps 4%. Doc Savage's light was still on. There was noise coming from the office. Shouting, of course. A man. Oh. Interesting. A man's voice she recognised. When she got close enough the smell confirmed it. The man that had kidnapped Veronica Dempsey was arguing loudly with her PhD supervisor after hours in her office.

Veronica shrugged it off and meandered past the office to the lab. She didn't know precisely why he had kidnapped her but she was sure he had his reasons. She had grown accustomed to taking things on faith: how the internet works, that hotdogs are edible, that nut allergies were the result of a government experiment in eugenics and, now, that if someone wanted to snoop in her lab and kidnap her he probably had a fairly good reason behind it. He had let her go so there was no harm done anyway. She didn't know why the same person would be shouting at and being shouted at by her boss, but she didn't have to take that particular event "on faith" on account of it falling squarely into the large and encompassing bracket of Really Not Caring Enough To Care. She had work to do.

We don't, so we can consider the lab violating events in more detail.

Chapter, the ThirtyNinth
For Completeness

Doc Savage has a back that is proportionally too long for her body. People were prone to find her less attractive than they might because of it, although they rarely knew why. Attractive traditionalism has no laws. More importantly, Doc Savage has a big mouth: 80 mm diameter (3.15" in old money), 90 millilitres volume, that is to say, 12.3 teaspoons and 2.5×10^{-3} bushels (which is the scientific way to write 0.0025 bushels). Her idea of keeping a secret is to only tell two dozen people and blog it. It, therefore, didn't take long for exactly the wrong sorts of people to become aware of it, it being Veronica Dempsey's Super Secret Wonder Drug.

The Story of Peter O'Shaughnessy

Peter O'Shaughnessy's mother didn't love him and called him 'lardass' when he was a child. As a result, PO'S bicycled till his ass was hard as granite and the shape of a Picasso masterpiece and slept with a thousand women. Nothing to this psychology lark.

He was employed by the number two pharmaceutical company in the UK. The number two pharma company wanted to be the number one pharma company so they could buy more private jets and a gold-plated brontosaurus. The plan to become Number

One had many fronts. Plan, the first: they rubbished the current number ones anonymously on the internet. At any one time there was a team of 20 on the mission 24 hours a day posting defamatory reports about adverse effects to drugs produced by the Current Number One Pharma Company, for example, "This teething gel made my baby's foot fall off!" and "This antibiotic made my fingernails grow fur! Avoid!" and "My girlfriend left me when I took this migraine tablet because she said I was no longer sexy! LFMF!". People will believe anything they read on the internet, particularly if it is ended with the wisdom of LFMF, which, in non-internet language translates as "learn from my fail". Plan, the second: outsource, obviously. Why pay a British worker £10 an hour when they can pay an Indian child 4p a year. It's nothing personal, it's economics. Plan, the third: industrial espionage. They kept their ear to the ground on any breakthrough drug discoveries, stole them and got them to patent first. A lot of tips came through the Internet Team. Peter O'Shaughnessy was coupled with the Doc Savage case. Looked very straightforward on paper. University missions were so much easier than competing pharma company missions who tended to have real security. Get in, hide, retrieve pertinent lab books, photograph said books, take information back to Number Two Company to fast track the drug through trials. Ta da. Plan, the fourth was to do actual work and make up their own drugs from scratch but that was tiresome and never worked.

Off Peter O'Shaughnessy set with his plan in action. He got in. No problem. Found the lab books. Problem. There was nothing of interest in them. They were hashing out old work. Badly. He looked again. Nope, still mediocre work. Nothing in them that lardass could use. He lost his temper and trashed the place. Hid. Then left, annoyed with a failed mission. He got airmiles on the company's current private jets when one of his acquisitions made patent and he was planning a trip to California to look at lipstick lesbians. Not now though, since it was a big fat waste of time. He memoed the office:

Big fat waste of time, unless we care about the cleaners. Should I follow them? Pete.

They memoed back:

Intel is good. Get on with it or don't come back. Stay away from the cleaners and do your job.

He broke into the Dempsey's, got as far as the loft and was accosted by a nutter who kept him locked up for the weekend, let him go and he walked into a moving artic lorry killing him instantly. He didn't go back to work.

Here endeth the tale of Peter O'Shaughnessy, the no good, lying, pathological cheating bastard and his attempt to steal VD's magnificent opium.

The Story of the Other Guy

A meeting was held that wasn't held in Veronica Dempsey's head and wasn't exclusively attended by blacks. Mostly white people with white hair sat around a table that was older than their combined age. They swirled brandy, chewed on cigars and made noises like 'myeah' before starting their sentences.

'Myeah, shocking news, this. Is it possible?' One said while swirling his cigar.

'Blarrb, I suppose. A lot of things are possible,' said another while chewing his brandy.

'Flarm, we'll need to take care of it,' said a third while munching glass, 'think of the proletarians. We can't have it! What if they start ... thinking?'

'Mrah! Send The Albino to investigate,' said the first and went for a nap.

The Albino was no such thing. He had dark hair, buzz cut but uncharacteristically soft, dark eyes and peach going on tan skin. What was the point of giving people secret handles that resembled them? Just made it easier for the enemy to pick them out of a line up. Thus, The Albino was not an albino. He worked for an invisible branch of the civil service who kept a lid on the cures for all the big diseases so there was less mouths to feed. This incident was a little outside their remit, but it made sense. If this wonder drug lived up to the rumours, hundreds of thousands of druggies would suddenly become sentient again and would want to work for a living in jobs that just did not exist. Better for them to keep them down.

Off The Albino set for the university. Someone had got there before him and given the place a damn good seeing to, probably the pharmaceutical sector, always keen to get a leg up by any means necessary but had the temper of a toddler not getting their own way. He read Doc Savage's emails and notes. Veronica Dempsey was at the heart of the matter so he went straight for her, kidnapping her for the total of two hours and 45 minutes before realising she wasn't going to lay down any chemical formulae and released her in a rare display of compassion. He planned on trailing her, but was so bored by her he gave up by the Saturday afternoon, thus missing the opportunity of trailing her to the West Country for an exceedingly interesting Sunday. Back to Doc Savage then, he decided. He went down the well-trodden path of seduction to get into her knowledge. What Veronica Dempsey heard as she walked past Doc Savage's office the night of her brother's nuptials was nothing more than a spat between her boss and her kidnapper (that is to say, her boss's new lover) over him not making the bed in the morning when he was last to get up. He was up to his neck in cover.

Having spent more than 18 minutes in the presence of Doc Savage, The Albino (or Frank as he introduced himself) was fairly confident she didn't have the wherewithal to get her drug to market, unless the almost impossible happened and a former Nobel Prize winner phoned her out the blue to see what she was up to.

Here endeth not the tale of The Albino (or Frank in the bedroom) and his quest to quash VD's merry opium.

*

There was a final faction about to get very interested in VD's magenta opium. He whose business would take a direct financial battering if her drug became a success, the local Mafia boss and all round humanitarian, Luigi. Here beginneth his part in the opera.

Chapter, the Fortieth
Conversation With The Dead, Part II

Veronica Dempsey was not a fugitive for the time being. Her illegal activities had ceased since the ground bones of the private investigator who inconsiderately died in her loft were sprinkled on the Styx, removing the last remnant of his being from the planet; no one mourned the loss of a pointy-toothed friend. All was well with her brain. The routine of life returned happily. It had missed her as she had missed it. They frolicked together for the first few days, enjoying the routine like they were experiencing it for the first time. Her life was uninterrupted for almost ten days, then the lab was broken into, again.

'FFS!' Davey Jones shouted when he saw the mess, again. That's yoof talk for 'for fuck's sake'. Under the circumstances swearing by abbreviation showed considerable restraint. He expected Doc Savage to be livid and for the people on the International Space Station to hear her shout about it. Instead she smiled wryly and said, 'Clean it up.' There were no words for how appreciative she was of having a student with total recall. Veronica Dempsey's Magenta Opium lab book was inside her mind. She remembered every addition of every chemical she made on every single day. She remembered what it smelled like and if it gave a better yield at 60 or 80 degrees or if stirred for four hours or overnight. She knew the shade of magenta it turned in the penultimate synthetic sequence depending on concentration. Doc Savage's enemies could turn the lab over as often as they wanted, her success was hidden deep in her star student's brain. The lab had been violated three times (only twice as far as the unobservant masses knew) and was becoming enough of a routine in itself for Veronica Rhythmic Dempsey to take it in her stride. So they cleaned up, again, losing a day's work, again.

That night the lab was hit again.

'FFS!' Davey Jones shouted, again, when he saw it, again. This time Doc Savage was a bit put out, but all she said, again, was 'Clean it up'. The more they tried to sabotage her the more she realised she was coming close to something big. She had already spent the Nobel Prize money.

Veronica Dempsey and Barta Savage had a private meeting. Again. Davey Jones and Pauline Burns, Doc Savage's lesser students, muttered about favouritism. It brought them closer together, but not close enough for Pauline Burns to let Davey Jones finger her. Doc Savage didn't notice the dip in morale. She had just, completely unexpectedly and out the blue, taken a phone call from a former Nobel Prize winner asking what she was up to. This as good as guaranteed her opiate would be produced and she would be knighted for services to the world. This last private meeting that BS and VD had was passing on the good news. The magnificent, merry magenta opium was to be taken out of Veronica's hands and given to the former Nobel Prize winner's industrial collaborators, ready and able to turn Doctor Barta Savage into a millionaire.

That night the lab was hit again. There was clearly a vendetta behind the recent string of attacks. Veronica was working late in the lab-abutting-office 7-14A. Planned one-offs of late nights at the computer were acceptable within the routine, and this was the one-off where she was about to commit to the ether instructions on making the World Changing Drug – when all of a sudden she heard the explosion and her brain melted to black.

*

Mr D. Ville sat on a bridge over the Styx, his legs swinging. He appeared to be wearing not a stitch of clothing. Veronica appeared to be standing on the river. Her clothes were smouldering and smelled of oxidised long chain hydrocarbons. 'Curious,' she said.

'I've been waiting for you,' Mr D. Ville said. 'How's life?'

'Short,' she replied, 'How's death?'

'Dry. Any regrets?'

'What do you mean "dry"?'

'Water, water everywhere. But not a drop to drink. Any regrets?'

'Why can't you drink it?' She asked.

'It burns. Any regrets?'

'Is it salty? Acidic? Lime?'

'Bacteria laden, they chew on your throat as you swallow. Any regrets?'

'What sort of bacteria?'

'The usual sort, common or garden bacteria. Any regrets?'

'Procaryotes? Eucaryotes?'

'When I say "any regrets" do you somehow hear "any more inane questions"?'

'Any what?'

'Regrets.'

'Not off hand,' she said after considering the question for a moment. Did she regret not having had sex before death? Did she regret working late the night someone blew up her lab? Did she regret decomposing Mr D. Ville in a bathtub in the West Country rather than the Lake District? Did she regret never having been inside the Great Pyramid? Did she regret never mixing chocolate and strawberry sauce on her ice-cream? Did she regret not getting to say goodbye to her dad? Did she regret never having composed a piece of music? Did she regret never reading Shakespeare? Did she regret not inventing a bionic body that would survive a nuclear blast? Did she regret having spent 27 hours to complete Majora's Mask? Did she regret not seeing an eclipse from space? Did she regret watching that one episode of Big Brother, series four? Regrets seemed entirely pointless now.

A troll jumped out from under the bridge, scaring the pants off Veronica. 'There, there,' Mr D. Ville said to the hulking beast, 'she's not for you yet.'

'What do you mean "yet"? Am I not dead?' Veronica asked, only slightly relieved.

'Why do you think you're dead?'

'Because you are and we're talking.'

'Are we?' he asked.

'Yes,' she said wondering what she'd done on earth to be sent to a hell like this. Aside from the obvious of being responsible for the death of the man now tormenting her with primary school psychology.

'But ⁀ e we?' he asked.

'When can I go?' she asked.

'When you're ready,' he told her.

'I'm ready,' she said.

'When I say you're ready. And when we reach a deal.'

Veronica started to sink into the syrupy Styx. She tried to make herself lighter but her ankles were now below the water line. Now half her calves. She thought light thoughts: 99 red balloons, Maltesers, skimmed milk. No good, she was up to her knees.

'Can you help me?'

'I can,' he smiled.

'Will you?' she clarified.

'If I touch you I will send you back, but I will keep the essence of you here with me. Fair's fair.'

The troll watched on and salivated, raising the level of the river. The wetness was now touching her butt cheeks and creeping ever upwards. It was making a steady pace up her body, about 20 cm a minute. She had in the region of three minutes to do something, certainly no more than four. Her legs were fixed in an upright position: there would be no swimming out of this one. She couldn't swim in practise anyway. Certainly, she had mastered the theory behind it (don't drown), but swam with the efficiency of a boulder with a rock chained to it. She had to touch him soon. She had to hold the hand that she had stripped back to the bone then went smashity happy with a hammer, pulverising the bones to powder. The hand outstretched to her looked intact. He had been a fairly pleasant host under the circumstances. He had the right to be a bit snappish with her after what she did to him. The water splashed at her face.

'It burns the throat, remember,' he said.

Veronica swallowed the dark fluid – in death, the Styx; on Earth, thick smoke. Much to her surprise she chose to live. She reached out to touch the man whose death she had been (at least partially, philosophically speaking) responsible for, sealing her pact with a demidevil … A figure materialised, too late, bearing an uncanny resemblance to Danny Kaye and shouting in Danny Kaye's actual voice, 'Don't send her back!'

The next thing she heard was a male voice close by her head, talking, but it wasn't Mr D. Ville. It was … Davey Jones?

'Veronica wake up!' Davey Jones yelled.

She woke up. She looked at him. She looked around. She was moving. The back of a van? The back of an ambulance. Much better.

'I nearly lost you,' Davey Jones said, water collecting in his eyes. He took her hand, bent over her and kissed her. She kissed him back, though she couldn't really remember how she knew him. Still, if you can't kiss a stranger in the back of an ambulance, when can you kiss a stranger? Seemed like a normal response.

That was clue number one that something was wrong.

Chapter, the FortyFirst
The First Day

Yet another mystery went officially unsolved by the friendly ineffectual neighbourhood fuzz. Davey Jones, who decided to keep an eye on the ever suspicious Veronica (What's She Up To Now?) Dempsey, was the only eye witness. His eye witness report was of two black-clad ghosts who moved through and round objects in an inhuman way. They were two beings that moved as one, almost as if telepathically linked. If the shiny-buttoned-policepersons did link the pair of hooligans to the reports that the local Godfather was currently body-guarded by two black-belted ninjas, no one took it up directly with Luigi. Now the lab was destroyed there was hardly likely to be any other attacks, best not to stir up trouble with Luigi, really. Besides, it could have been an accident. The eye witness was too distraught to be a reliable eye witness.

Davey Jones turned into a hero in his hour of fate. The lab was burning ferociously and mini explosions were shattering glass down the length of the room. There was no shortage of fuel so the fire grew hotter and released toxic fumes by the lungful. His first instinct was to run. The fire was too big, too hot and too full of plasmic death to hang around. No one would know he had been there, no one would have judged him for running away. His brain's self preservation shouted for him to get out, his brain's compassion told him to stay and help. The lifeforce took over and he ran to the stairs.

'FFS,' he muttered when his body stopped without his brain telling it to. He turned back, compassion winning out over preservation. Take that science! He had to cross close to eight feet of burning laboratory to get to the office door where Veronica was. He wrapped himself in the fire blanket kept with safety in mind at the door and ran straight for the office. The first big explosion had knocked the door clean off its hinges and shattered the computer screens in the office. Veronica lay on the floor either unconscious or dead and very bloody. He dragged her through the fire and the flames to the relative safety of the corridor. He heard the sirens and knew they were going to be okay. He kept dragging her till the air was breathable and men in fire retardant mustard yellow suits escorted them outside just before the final explosion which took out the entire floor.

In the ambulance Veronica regained consciousness for a moment. Someone was shouting. Who was he? Where was she? Who?

'You're okay,' he said, 'there was an explosion, but you're okay.'

'You rescued me?' she asked.

He nodded and tears of relief filled his smoke stung eyes. She was actually okay. That was the second clue.

'Thank you,' she said, pulled his head towards hers and kissed him, then passed out with her lips pressing his.

Nothing in real life ever ended in a kiss for him. He was, therefore, either fantasizing (unlikely due to the real pain in his chest and back) or she wasn't actually okay.

She wasn't actually okay.

There was some brain damage. Her cast-iron mind was pitted and holed. With a lot of effort she could remember her name and that she had a brother. She knew she did something sciencey but couldn't think what, why or how. People visited. She recognised her dad. She didn't recognise her boss, who had to be removed by security for attacking Veronica and babbling on about being owed a Nobel Prize; words couldn't begin to describe how angry she was that Veronica Dempsey did not keep any notes at all on her important work, although she had pages and pages of Friedel-Crafts Alkylation Crap. She formed an unbreakable bond with Davey Jones, the boy who went back for her. She didn't really remember him from before the accident, but he had saved her life and she was grateful. After she had re-met everyone for the first time she remembered them the next time she saw them without prompting. Her memory was functioning at its usual high capacity, it was just starting from the accident onwards. Mr D. Ville kept her memories in his pocket in the Styx, but he gave her the recognition of her dad and brother since she technically didn't murder him and he was feeling lenient. He reformatted her mind. Fate's big plans for her washed away as she drowned in the Styx. The hope for the world that this insignificant girl carried in her brain was lost on the river bed. The human race was spared, for the now, the paradigm shift it would have to undertake with her Magenta Opium. Its choices were deferred. Its agenda remained uncomplicated by her.

Veronica Dempsey wasn't scared by what she didn't know any more. She was quite excited at the thought of reading books again and watching movies again but enjoying it as if she'd never read or seen them before. Chances were she hadn't read or seen them before anyway since she'd only ever seen two movies in her whole life (Big Fish[11] and The Matrix[12]) and read exactly no books that weren't categorised 'textbook'.

---

[11] The all star cast in Tim Burton's typical Tim Burton-style movie Big Fish make this movie almost perfect, with sterling performances all round and the best Tim Burton-style directing. Some beautiful moments make this worth a watch if you have 120 minutes to spare, but be aware that the movie is less than the sum of its parts. The relevant ASIN is B0001HK0RA.

[12] See page 90, footnote 6 for a discussion on The Matrix.

There's nothing like nearly dying to help you know how to live, and Veronica Dempsey was no exception. Every decision she made was based on the information at hand, not a preconception. She ate new foods, she chatted for the sake of it, she kissed Davey Jones a lot and she never again worried about tinkers stealing her letterbox.

Only the loft knew what was to come for the brain-damaged all the way to happiness girl and it wasn't for telling.

Chapter, the FortySecond
42

Life.
The Universe.
Everything[13].

---

[13] For a detailed explanation of 42 being the answer to life, the universe and everything (if indeed that was the question), the reader is directed towards Douglas Adams's The Hitchhiker's Guide to the Galaxy: The Trilogy of Four. For reading purposes, see ISBN: 0330492047, or if you fancy the televisual event, this author recommends (without bias) the BBC version (ASIN: B00005YUNJ) or if you really must then you could check out Hollywood's attempt here: ASIN B000A283AW (it's actually pretty good).

Dr Sharon Baillie (www.sharonbaillie.com) lives in the west coast of Scotland with her husband and two children.

Sharon has had short stories published in *Morpheus Tales* (a magazine of horror, science fiction and fantasy) and the *Reader's Digest* website (notably lacking in horror, science fiction and fantasy). If you search Sharon E Baillie online you'll get a selection of her published chemical works, although that advice should only be followed if you really want to know about some nifty novel chemistry.

Lightning Source UK Ltd.
Milton Keynes UK
UKOW041220140413

209185UK00001B/5/P

9 781614 690337